A GRAVE WELCOME

BLYTHE BAKER

❀ Created with Vellum

1

Stepping off the gangplank and touching solid ground for the first time in three weeks, I felt as though I was discovering a new continent. I was Magellan finding the East Indies, Roald Amundsen landing at the North Pole. Of course, London had been long discovered before the likes of Rose Beckingham set foot there, but that thought didn't dampen my excitement. I had arrived.

I looked back up at the hulking mass of the ship behind me. The RMS *Star of India* had borne me over rough seas, both figuratively and literally, and I was grateful to her for bearing the journey so well.

"Watch it!"

A woman carting a steamer trunk and two rambunctious children plowed into my shoulder, nearly knocking me back. I stopped to straighten myself, adjusting the brim of my beige cloche hat over my curls and smoothing out the travel creases in my tea gown. The dress had felt perfectly adequate for the weather in India, but the air in London had a chill to it. The wind bit against my exposed skin.

"Is there no better place for you to stand?"

A man with a twirled mustache stood only a few feet away with his arms full of luggage, sneering down at me so I wouldn't be able to miss the fact that I was directly in his path and being an utter nuisance. My cheeks flamed with embarrassment and I scrambled to get out of his way and away from the passengers disembarking the ship. Everyone had seemed so carefree while we were at sea—even with a murder investigation ongoing for most of the voyage—but now everyone looked harried. They scurried away from the ship and into the maze of the city like each one was already late for a meeting.

I turned on my heel, spinning in a full circle in search of Mr. and Mrs. Worthing, the couple who had acted as my chaperones for the duration of the voyage from Bombay to London. In all honesty, they had done little in the way of protecting me. Under their care, I still managed to unknowingly befriend a murderer and nearly be murdered by the same man. However, I couldn't blame them for that. I chose to dive head first into the investigation of who had killed Ruby Stratton, which placed me in a considerable amount of danger. In fact, the majority of the ship's passage had been spent trying to get away from the Worthings so I could investigate. But even still, I wanted to bid them farewell. I needed to thank them for their kindness and generosity.

As more and more passengers continued to move down the gangplank and fill the area surrounding the dock, it became more unlikely I would find the Worthings. Surely, they hadn't left without seeing me one last time? Mrs. Worthing had pulled me in for a cursory hug on our way out of the cabin, and Mr. Worthing had hurried her along, insistent on the fact we would have time to say goodbye once we were on land. But now, they were nowhere to be found.

Pulling my modest steamer trunk along behind me, I weaved my way through the crowd of people reuniting with family members and asking for directions towards their destination in the city. The crush of people didn't feel unfamiliar. The noisy, crowded streets of Bombay had prepared me for that. However, the pale faces were striking. Everything about London—based on the little I'd seen so far—seemed pale in comparison to India. The sky was a thick gray color, hanging over the stone city like fleece. Where India had been golden sunshine and red dirt and tanned skin, London was faded and foggy and cold. A pang of sudden homesickness sprung up in my chest for the warm and vivacious country I would likely never see again.

I shook my head and tried to look at the city with new eyes. I couldn't wander around London in awe and wonder. I was supposed to have been here before. More than that, I had to create the illusion that I'd *lived* in London before. The slate gray city should feel like coming home. I closed my eyes and tried to channel the other Rose's enthusiasm for the place. All the time I knew her in India, she told me repeatedly how much she missed London.

"You would love the shopping there," she said one day while we sat on her bed, fanning ourselves from the heat of the Indian summer. "Custom-made hats and dresses in any fabric you could imagine."

"You can find custom-made hats and dresses in Bombay," I countered, fingering the hem of my bright yellow sun dress.

Rose fell back on the bed, her blankets nearly swallowing her up. "It's not the same. London is where fashion lives and breathes, Nellie. By the time the latest fashions arrive here, everyone in London is on to something new. I can't wait to get home."

The memory fell upon me like a stone, crushing the breath out of me. In that moment it was hard to believe Rose could be dead. A tear fell from the corner of my eye, and I swiped at it with my gloved hand, dabbing away the moisture so as not to smudge my makeup. I had assumed Rose's identity five weeks ago, yet I still felt entirely inadequate. I didn't have her dramatic flair, and I worried everyone could see that. Of course, having supposedly survived what had killed her parents, Rose would have good reason to seem less enthusiastic now.

Lost in thought, I'd wandered across the street from the ship and down a narrow side street. Mrs. Worthing would have opted for the least busy passage into the city, so I knew I had a better chance of finding her and her husband there than on the main roads. Still, the stream of cars and passengers coming away from the docks filled the street and the sidewalks. I was a helpless fish caught in the current. I swiveled my head, standing on my toes to try and see above the crush of the crowd, but finally, I sunk down onto my feet and let myself be washed away.

Eventually, I came to a wide bridge where I was able to duck out of the walkway and stand in the shade of the arch. Since the day had already been gray and overcast, the underside of the bridge was nothing but inky shadows. An alley ran alongside the structure and it looked to cross behind a row of buildings and open onto another busy street that ran down to where the ship had docked. Perhaps the Worthings had gone down a busy street in search of me just as I had gone down a vacant street in search of them.

I could see more people with luggage, clearly having come from the ship, up ahead, but I also saw regular Londoners. People going about their daily commute. Men loading cargo ships, boys waving rags and shouting their price for a shoe shine. The constant din of voices and cars whirred around me like a machine and I thought how easy it would be to get lost in such a large city. Then, a voice cut through the noise, closer than the others.

A man stood in the shadow of a low, stone building, his back to me. He wore a dark coat and a fashionable fedora hat. His arms were waving animatedly and the wind carried his voice my way. He was angry, that much was clear.

I took another step forward and a second man appeared just behind the corner. He was shorter than the other man, his face indistinct in the darkness, nothing but hard lines and blotchy cheeks. He had a thick mess of dark hair on top of his head that he tried to hide under a dark gray flat cap.

"You're angry for nothing, Frederick," the one in the flat cap said. "I didn't do anything wrong."

I could hear a scowl in the other man's voice. "What kind of fool do you take me for? I saw the two of you cozied up together."

"Your imagination is very vivid, then, because no such thing happened."

The man in the fedora lunged out at the other, pushing him hard in the chest so that he stumbled backward.

I jumped at the suddenness of the attack, falling back into the stone arch of the bridge, catching myself with the palms of my hands. A jagged rock scraped the back of my neck as I fell and I winced at the sharp pain.

Then, the shouting stopped. The voices that had, only a moment before, been reaching a crescendo, had gone completely quiet. I pressed myself against the bridge, hoping they wouldn't see me. Why hadn't I stayed near the ship? I'd been in London for a matter of minutes and already I'd found myself in a deserted alley in the company of two angry men.

I counted to thirty and held in my sigh of relief when the voices resumed.

"You don't want a quarrel with me. It will not end well for you."

I couldn't see who had offered that ominous warning as I was already halfway down the alley, headed in the direction I'd originally come from, towards the protection of the crowded street.

2

Stepping back onto the crowded street felt like experiencing daylight for the first time after a month of darkness. The weather, which had only moments before felt cold and gloomy, suddenly warmed my cool skin.

It felt as though everyone I passed knew where I'd just been. I took deep breaths, trying to calm my rapidly beating heart. As it always did during times of stress, my hand reached for the locket around my neck. The locket I'd kept pressed against my heart for years, carrying it with me always. Except, for the first time since I could remember, I grabbed at empty air. Forgetting all decency, I pulled at the collar of my dress and looked down my front, but the inside of my gown was empty. Still, my fingers reached for the clasp at the back of my neck. Once again, there was nothing. I'd lost it.

My feet stopped moving. I stood frozen on the street, disregarding the shouts of the crowd around me, people hurrying through their lives, ignoring my heartbreak. How had I lost it? When?

Then came the memory of jumping back into the stone.

The sharp pain at the back of my neck. I'd lost it in the alley. Immediately, I turned on my heel to make my way back to the alley, all fear of the fighting men lost to my determination to once again have my locket safely around my neck.

"Rose, dear!"

Mrs. Worthing was waving a handkerchief above her head as she walked down the sidewalk towards me, Mr. Worthing trailing behind. Her lips were pursed together, her cheeks red from the wind.

"Where did you wander off to once we disembarked the ship?" she asked, pulling me briefly into her arms for a hug. She did not wait for me to answer. "I know you are a grown woman and not actually in need of our guidance, but we swore to see you safely to London and our job is not complete until you are happily in the company of your relatives."

Mr. Worthing walked ahead of us, talking over his shoulder as he went. "We need to get back to the passenger entry office. Last night I put a call through to your uncle, Rose. Lord Ashton seems to be a fine man. Fine man. He said there would be a car waiting for you at the port's entry office once you left the ship."

I wanted to turn back and find my locket. I wanted to forget about the London branch of the Beckingham family and the Worthings and search for the necklace, but I couldn't. The locket's importance was wrapped up in my own personal mission, and without spilling all of my secrets, no one would understand why it meant so much to me. Without the Beckinghams and the Worthings believing my story entirely, I wouldn't be able to help anyone. Assuming Rose's identity and coming to London would be for nothing. So, for the sake of my ultimate goal, I followed the Worthings back towards the ship.

"There is no need to be nervous, Rose," Mrs. Worthing said, squeezing my elbow. "Your family will be so pleased to see you. I'm sure they've been beside themselves with grief and worry."

It was then I decided it wouldn't do any harm to tell the Worthings what I'd seen. Mr. Worthing could notify a police officer and they could be told where they might return my locket should it be found by any passersby.

"Oh, I am not nervous about seeing the Beckinghams again," I said, though this was nothing close to the truth. I was terrified of meeting Rose's relations, considering it would be for the first time, even though I was meant to have known them my whole life. "I did not plan to mention it, but I can't push the thought from my mind a second longer. Moments before you found me on the road behind us, I had just run away from a rather disturbing encounter."

"Run away?" Mrs. Worthing asked, no doubt thinking of how unladylike I had looked while doing it.

"Disturbing encounter?" Mr. Worthing echoed, concern etched in the lines of his face.

I turned to him and nodded solemnly. "Yes, I believe I witnessed an attempted robbery of some kind. Two men were shouting at one another in an alley and one man lunged at the other. Fearing for my own safety, I ran from the scene and did not see the outcome, but it looked like a violent altercation."

Mrs. Worthing pressed a gloved hand to her open mouth. "Good heavens! Are you hurt?"

I reached for her hands and held them in my own, squeezing her fingers in a reassuring manner. "No, Mrs. Worthing. I am perfectly safe. Excepting a gold locket I dropped in the excitement, I am perfectly well."

"Did you get a good view of either of the men?" Mr.

Worthing asked, standing on the tips of his feet, trying to see above the crowd, as if he thought the men I spoke of might be creeping up on us. "We should probably report what you saw, before those fellows can do any harm."

No sooner had he said the words than Mrs. Worthing reached her hand into the flow of traffic around us and pulled a passing police officer out by his elbow as though she were drawing a fish from a river barehanded. "Sir, we have a crime to report."

The officer, a young man with pale hair and an even paler face, straightened his hat upon his head and stared at the Worthings, a look of bewilderment spread across his face. Then he looked over at me, and his expression softened. His eyes turned up in surprise and his lips fell apart. A blush crept into his cheeks.

"What seems to be the trouble?" he asked, not taking his eyes from me.

"Tell him what you saw, Rose." Mrs. Worthing shifted from one foot to the other, trying to gain the attention of the officer, but he kept his gaze fixed on me. "She encountered a violent altercation nearby. Two men."

The officer looked from me to Mrs. Worthing and back again. "Is this true?"

I nodded, my hand moving absentmindedly to my cheek. I felt the lightly scarred skin over my dented cheekbone, and turned away from him. "Yes, it's true. The men were two streets back in an alley."

The officer looked over my head and diagonally, as if he could see through buildings and locate the men without taking another step. After a few seconds, he tipped his hat and smiled at me. "I'll look into it."

"Thank you," I said, having forgotten the reason I'd told the Worthings about the altercation at all. Luckily, Mrs.

Worthing couldn't be so easily distracted by a smooth, handsome face.

"Rose also lost a locket near the scene. If you discover it, have it returned to Miss Rose Beckingham at the home of Lord and Lady Ashton," she said, emphasizing the names of my aunt and uncle clearly.

His eyebrows rose in recognition and with one final smile and nod of his hat, the officer cut a path down the road, headed for the scene.

BY THE TIME we reached the ship again, the crowd around the dock had thinned. It was no surprise everyone had cleared out quickly. The wind off the ocean was icy and sharp, slicing through my clothes and giving me chills. Luckily, the passenger entry office had plush chairs and a fire roaring in the hearth while we waited for the car. I couldn't remember ever seeing a fireplace in use while in India.

"I'm going to be sad to see you go, Rose" Mrs. Worthing said, dabbing at her dry eyes with a handkerchief.

I didn't doubt her sincerity. On the contrary, in the weeks I'd come to know Mrs. Worthing, I knew she had a very large heart and rarely said anything she didn't mean entirely. However, she also had a flare for the dramatic. Mopping up her pretend tears simply made the moment more memorable, which was why she'd done it.

"We will see her again, dear," Mr. Worthing said, patting his wife's shoulder and looking over her head to find me and offer a reassuring smile. "Just because our voyage is ending does not mean our friendship must. We will all be living in the same city, after all."

I nodded in agreement. "Yes, absolutely. I won't allow us to never see one another again."

"You'll come for dinner, then?" Mrs. Worthing asked, her voice full of hope.

"Only if you promise to dine with me once I'm settled into my own home," I said.

"You won't live with the Beckinghams?" Mrs. Worthing asked. "I assumed you would want to live with family for the time being."

I shrugged. "I suppose only time will tell. Perhaps I will decide I enjoy the Beckinghams and test their good faith."

Mrs. Worthing pulled me in for another hug and pressed her lips against my hair. "I have cherished our time together these last few weeks. It would take someone of very little good faith to tire of you."

"A car has arrived," Mr. Worthing said, breaking up the emotional hug to point to the curb just in front of the office. I turned towards the window and away from Mrs. Worthing just in the nick of time. I was moments away from shedding very real tears. I had so few people in the world who cared about me. It made me happy to think I could add the Worthings to that list. Of course, they believed me to be Rose Beckingham, daughter of a deceased British government official in India, but that seemed like an unnecessary detail.

"Oh, this is all happening so quickly," Mrs. Worthing said, wringing her hands. "Do you have everything you need, Rose?"

I looked down at my small steamer trunk. It was the only thing I'd taken with me when we left India. After the attack that killed the true Rose Beckingham and her parents, it had been too dangerous for me to go back to the house where they had lived for so many years, for fear of another attack.

I'd bought what I needed before leaving India with the promise that I would receive my inheritance from my family back in London and have plenty of money to replace whatever possessions I wished.

"I believe so," I said.

Mrs. Worthing nodded her head and glanced around the small room, double-checking that was true. Then, she stood in front of me and placed her hands on my shoulders. "You are a brave young woman, Rose Beckingham. I can't begin to imagine the horrors you've experienced these last few weeks. I only hope your future is much brighter than your recent past."

Once again, tears welled behind my eyes and I swallowed them back, my throat thick. "Thank you, Mrs. Worthing."

Mr. Worthing patted my back quickly, and I glanced up at him to see a slight mist in his eyes, though he was clearly trying to ignore it. "Well. Enough with the goodbyes. We will see one another again. We need to get you to the car before the driver leaves you behind."

He took my trunk and pushed on my lower back, leading me towards the door. Suddenly, a nervous ball of energy grew in my chest. The next phase of my plan was beginning, and I wasn't as confident as I'd been at the start. Fooling the Worthings into believing I was Rose Beckingham had been easy. They hadn't known Rose and had only seen her in old photographs. Rose's relations, however, would have a much better memory of her features and habits. They had shared a family history with Rose that I was not a part of. Would I be able to fake my way through old memories and familial anecdotes?

As we stepped onto the sidewalk, a chauffeur slid from the driver's seat and moved to meet us at the front of the car, his hands behind his back. He wore a dark gray jacket with two rows of buttons cutting vertically down the front, paired with matching pants, and a high pair of black boots. He had a gray cap pushed back on his head, framing his tanned cheekbones and wavy auburn hair.

"Miss Rose?" he asked, already bending his upper body in a low bow without awaiting confirmation. "I'm sorry to be late. I had a bit of trouble finding where I was meant to park."

The man seemed full of nervous energy. His hands folded and unfolded behind his back and his eyes darted from me to the Worthings continuously, as if unable to rest on any one face for too long. I wondered whether his anxiety came from fear of disappointing me or his employers. I hoped it was the former. I wanted the Beckinghams to be abundantly kind people. The sort of people who would be much too afraid of offending anyone to ask whether they were actually who they said they were.

"That is perfectly all right. We only just got here, anyway," I said. "I, too, had a hard time finding where I was supposed to meet you."

The chauffeur smiled his appreciation and reached for my trunk, which Mr. Worthing handed over readily. As he loaded my luggage in the back of the car, Mrs. Worthing looped her arm through mine and walked with me to the curb.

"I am sorry for the circumstances under which we met, but I am glad we got to know one another, Rose," Mrs. Worthing said, placing her gloved hand on my forearm and squeezing.

"As am I," I said, squeezing her hand in return.

She beamed up at me and then pulled away as the chauffeur moved to open the passenger side door. But before he could, I saw a red smear on the silver handle. I recognized the rust color immediately.

Suddenly, I found myself beneath the familiarly warm sun of India, a cloud of dust enveloping me as I looked around, trying to understand why my ears were ringing, why my eyes burned. The people who had only moments before filled the street around our car, making the journey through Simla a slow one, had disappeared. The laughter and conversation I'd been ignoring in favor of my own thoughts had silenced. I turned my head, a simple movement that made me feel as though I were swimming through quicksand. Rose had been sitting beside me, but when I was finally able to focus on the spot where she'd been, I realized her seat was empty. My friend had disappeared to be replaced by a puddle of blood on the leather seat. The red liquid dripped from the upholstery onto the floor in thick rivulets. I leaned forward to make sense of it, not yet recognizing the horror before me. As I did, I noticed a hand in the backseat. Her hand. The long, delicate fingers of my friend, disconnected from her body.

I shook my head, trying to separate myself from the horror. I took deep breaths of the cool, London air and tried to focus on the movement around me. On the normalcy of everyday life continuing on despite my flashback.

"Are you feeling all right, Miss?"

The chauffeur's nerves had clearly been replaced by concern. His eyebrows were pulled together as he stooped down to peer into my face.

I blinked several times slowly. I wanted to respond, but everything felt far away, even my own thoughts. I turned to find the Worthings, but they were no longer behind me. They were halfway down the street, walking arm in arm.

"Miss?"

I looked back at the door handle, but the blood from moments before was gone. The Chauffeur pulled the door open further and used a bare hand to direct me inside.

"Are you ready?" he asked.

My face reddened with embarrassment. "Yes, of course. I'm sorry."

I stepped into the car and let the chauffeur shut the door behind me. As he walked around the back of the car and hopped into the driver's seat, I took deep, calming breaths.

I couldn't allow myself to fall into my memories in that way. I needed to keep up appearances, which included not letting everyone around me think I was mad.

The blood had been in my imagination. Being back in a large city and climbing into a car had simply pushed my memories to the surface, jumbling them with the present. If there had been blood visible on the door, the Worthings would have seen it. The chauffeur would have seen it. Someone would have mentioned the oddity. But no one had, which meant I must have imagined it. That was the only logical explanation.

"All set, Miss?" the chauffeur asked over his shoulder as he put the car into gear.

The next time I got out of the car, I would be meeting Rose's relatives. My relatives. The people who could destroy the disguise I'd kept up this long. The people who could make everything I'd done up to this point useless. I took a deep breath, closed my eyes, and reminded myself of my ultimate goal. If I failed and the Beckinghams barred me from their home and Rose's inheritance, I wouldn't be the only person in dire straits.

My hand reached for the locket that was no longer around my neck, and when I found nothing there, my fingers instead brushed along my collar bone. I thought of the small scrap of paper I'd carried inside the locket for so long. Two words, scribbled in haste and faded with time: *help me.*

I leaned forward, placing my hand on the back of the front seat and smiled. "Yes, I'm ready."

I only hoped the words were true. I hoped I was ready. Then, I whispered to the young boy who had written that message. "Only a little longer now."

3

As we drove through the city, every second coming closer and closer to the moment I would meet Rose's surviving relations, I began to panic. It wasn't an easy fear to swallow, the kind I could bite back and hide behind a smile. No, it began in my chest and spread to my limbs. The hairs on my arms stood up, my fingers shook with every movement, my foot bounced and danced erratically no matter how I crossed my legs and tried to pin it down. My brain raced through a series of different, yet horrible scenes in which the Beckinghams discovered my deception and had me arrested or attacked me. Each imagining more gruesome than the last.

On the ship, as I continued to fool the Worthings and everyone else on board with my British accent, I had become cocky. Until, of course, Dr. Rushforth had discovered me. In the moments before I accused him of murder and he killed himself, he told me that my false accent had slipped. He'd noticed it right away, and knew I was not the heiress I claimed to be. What if I slipped again?

More than that, Rose had lived in London for years. She

would be closely familiar with the sights and sounds, the food and customs. Whereas, I had grown up in New York and India, neither of which had much in common with England. And the only people I'd been in contact with who had any familiarity with Rose had been the Worthings, who knew her only from old photographs. What would her family members think? Her aunt and uncle would certainly be more familiar with the delicate shape of Rose's face, the plumpness of her lips, the intricate number of ways in which she was more prim than I could ever hope to be.

During the time I'd spent in India as Rose's servant and close friend, I'd learned to mimic her accent as well as I would ever be able to manage. I'd become familiar with her distant relatives during late night conversations under the covers and while on afternoon strolls. I'd read the letters her aunt and uncle sent. I knew about her cousins, Edward, Catherine, and Alice. But would that cursory information be enough?

I'd received one letter after the explosion that killed Rose and her parents. Rose's uncle, Lord Ashton, sent for her—for me. He said the family would love to see her again, that she did not need to worry for a second about finances because her inheritance awaited. By that point, I had already been mistaken for Rose by the doctors and the Worthings, and I'd gone along with the falsehood, too confused and scared to disagree. But it wasn't until I'd opened the letter that I had committed to the idea. That I had decided my true self, Nellie Dennet, died in the crash, and Rose had lived.

"Is it nice to be back in the city?" the chauffeur asked, drawing me from my thoughts.

I looked out the window, at the gray buildings and pale people and houses flashing past. "Yes," I said, nodding my head even though the driver could not see me. "It's wonderful to be back."

"I'm sure a lot has changed since you were last here," he said.

That was true. A lot had changed. England had gone to war and won. Families were torn apart, buildings were destroyed, the economy suffered. The London I was seeing through my window looked very different from the one Rose had last known. Anyone would understand if I couldn't remember specific buildings or houses. If I forgot the names of some of my old friends. No one would blame me, especially after the devastating loss of both of my parents. After the trauma of surviving the explosion that had destroyed my family. No one would be bold enough to challenge my memory when my mind had been so irrevocably altered by the attack. Besides, Rose hadn't seen London in ten years, meaning no one in London had seen Rose since she was thirteen. Ten years was a considerable amount of time, especially when one was changing from a girl into a woman. Rose's delicate face could have filled in as she matured. Her narrow shoulders could have broadened to look less like her mother's and more like her father's. And the accident. The shrapnel had scarred my cheek and dented the bone. No one would comment on the differences of my face from that of the Rose they had known as a girl, not when I wore the wound of the accident so openly. It wouldn't be proper to remind me of the horror of that day.

I scooted closer to the window, practically pressing my face up against the glass. Finally allowing myself to gawk at the city. To take London in with wide, curious eyes. "Yes, it's quite different. I almost do not recognize it," I said with a smile.

THE CHAUFFEUR TURNED onto a wide road with large brick houses lining either side. Huge trees with gray trunks and moss green leaves stretched across the sky, forming a canopy that shaded the entire block.

"Miss Rose, the Beckinghams live just there," the chauffeur said, pointing several houses ahead of us, towards a white stone house that sat in the middle of the street.

I didn't acknowledge the comment, since it was information I was already supposed to know. But I did lean out my window to get a better look.

The line of trees blocked my view of the house, so the first thing I saw was the gate—wrought iron and covered in a flowering ivy that wound around the bars and stretched up one corner of the house. Finally, the car stopped in front of the house, and I saw it in all its glory.

Rose had told me her aunt and uncle, the London Beckinghams, were also the Lord and Lady of Ashton. The house certainly spoke to the grandness of their position. An arched iron gate opened to a brick path that led to the front steps. The stairs came outward in a half-circle and were framed on either side by twin pillars that stretched up the front of the three-story house. Three large windows were set into every floor, pointed pediments topping each one. The structure looked cold and commanding, but the garden in front gave it some warmth. Flowers and shrubs were planted in rows that lined the house on either side of the porch.

"The whole house is for the Beckingham family?" I asked.

The chauffeur had parked the car and come around to open my door. He looked at me with a question in his eyes for only a minute before turning his face to a neutral mask.

"Yes, Miss Rose. The servants live in the attics, but otherwise the house is just for the family."

I nodded, trying to hide my embarrassment at having asked such a silly question. It was something Rose would have already known. I couldn't allow my curiosity to betray me.

Before I could spend too long dwelling on my slipup, the wooden front door opened and one by one, the Beckinghams poured from the house and down the front walkway.

"Rose, dear," the woman I presumed to be Lady Ashton said. She had long dark hair that had been pulled into a tight, intricate knot at the base of her head. She wore a cream gown that covered her from collarbone to ankles with a black ribbon tied around the tiny circumference of her waist. A bucket hat shaded her eyes from the gray daylight. "I hope you had a pleasant journey?"

The chauffeur moved past me, carrying my luggage to the front door, and I felt the weight of the moment hit me. The family was pouring outside where they would get a good look at me for the first time. If I messed up now, upon first meeting them, it could be the end of everything. I swallowed down the panic that threatened to burst out of me and stretched my dry lips into a smile.

"Yes, Aunt Eleanor. I had a very pleasant journey," I said, speaking slowly so my accent was sure not to falter. I also decided not to mention the murder aboard the ship or the confrontation I'd had with the killer. I would wait until later to share that story, if ever. Being involved in a murder investigation wasn't a normal hobby for an heiress, so it was best left unsaid.

Behind Eleanor Beckingham was a blond girl with a short bob hairstyle who appeared to be around my age. She wore a lacy blue dress that was loose around her waist, making her skin look luminous, with white t-strap heels. I recognized her immediately as Catherine Beckingham, the older of the Beckingham's two daughters. Rose had a photograph of the family on her wall, and though Catherine had been much younger in the photo, she seemed remarkably similar, if more womanly. Her younger sister, Alice, stood behind her. She had brown hair pulled back into a braid and freckles that dotted her nose and cheeks, making her appear younger than she actually was. She smiled and looked at me admiringly.

"Glad you arrived safely." Lord Ashton placed a hand on his wife's shoulder and offered up what I was sure he meant to be a smile, but what actually looked like little more than a grimace. He had blond hair the same shade as Rose's had been, and he wore a black suit that stretched across his wide shoulders. James Beckingham was a commanding man with an imposing voice and an even more imposing position. I imagined him confronting me about impersonating his niece, and the thought alone was enough to make my knees quake. I pushed the notion from my mind and smiled at him.

"Thank you, Uncle."

I wanted to say more, but my tongue felt dumb and heavy. It was as though every word could be a stumbling block, a sign that pointed to my deception.

Lady Ashton stepped forward and enveloped me in a motherly hug. She smelled like spices and warmth and I breathed her in. "We are, of course, so sorry for the loss of your parents. As you know, we loved them dearly and we cannot begin to imagine the pain you are feeling."

She spoke for the whole family that way, expressing her condolences as though they had all agreed how they felt beforehand and she was simply the mouthpiece. As she spoke, though, Catherine looked bored. She stared at the houses across the street as if willing them to burst into flames. Lord Ashton nodded along with his wife, but his facial expression remained distant and hard. Alice was the only family member, aside from Lady Ashton, who looked genuinely sorry. Her large brown eyes glazed over with tears as she looked up at me, her lips pulled down in a frown.

"Thank you all so much for your kindness," I said. "It has made this horrible time more bearable."

"I know the...um...*bodies* were not able to be shipped home for a proper burial, but we had a stone laid in memoriam. It's at Kensal Green cemetery, and I would love to take you there to visit whenever you are ready," Lady Ashton said. "And there is no hurry. I'm sure none of us can grasp the trauma you've experienced, so please take your time. We are just so glad that you are safe and unharmed. Losing your parents is a devastating blow, but if we had lost you, too...it would have been unbearable."

I smiled at her, gratitude and guilt threatening to overwhelm me. I knew I had a noble reason for impersonating Lady Ashton's niece, but part of me felt rotten for tricking her. She should be mourning Rose. Her name should also be written in Kensal Green cemetery. But instead, she was buried somewhere in India in a cheap grave that bore the name Nellie Dennet.

Lord Ashton turned to go inside, and the rest of the family followed him wordlessly. I brought up the rear, losing my nerve with each step. The house loomed over me, ominous against the heavy gray sky, and I wondered how I would ever make myself at home with a family of strangers. As soon as I stepped into the entrance, however, warmth enveloped me. A fireplace roared in the sitting room to the right of the front door and a large staircase led to the next level. The floors were a rich cherry color and plush rugs lay in the center of each room.

"This home is yours as much as any of ours," Lady Ashton said, moving next to me to wrap her arm around my waist and pull me further into the house. "I know your previous visits were as a guest, but now you are a cherished member of this family and I hope you will make yourself comfortable."

I smiled at her and looked up at the crystal chandelier hanging from the ceiling. A gold circle surrounded it with lace-like details filling the remainder of the ceiling. I had spoke to Mrs. Worthing of finding my own home, but suddenly it no longer felt like my main priority.

"I can take you upstairs and show you my room," Alice said, sidling up next to me, her long dress brushing against my calf.

"I'm sure our cousin is tired from her journey and would like to get settled in her own room."

I glanced up to see a young man with thick black hair standing on the staircase. One hand was resting on the banister, but the other was shoved deep into the pocket of his loose gray pants. He wore a plain white shirt with suspenders stretching over his shoulders and black oxfords.

"Where have you been, Edward? I called for you when Rose's car arrived out front," Lord Ashton said, his eyebrows pulled together in displeasure. "And why are you dressed like a servant?"

Edward ignored Lord Ashton's criticism and walked down the remainder of the stairs to the entrance hall. He stood a few inches taller than his father, but his frame was long and lean. He pulled his thin lips into a smile.

"It has been too long, Rose." Edward stepped forward and wrapped me in an awkward hug. His limbs felt stiff around me and I barely managed to raise my arms and pat his back before he was stepping away. "You look so different."

Immediately, I felt everyone's eyes appraising me, staring at the small scar on my left cheek. Even though the scar usually made me self-conscious, I hoped they were focusing on it now. As long as they were focused on the scar, they wouldn't be noticing the way my features looked different from those of the girl they'd once known.

"As do you, Edward," I said, ignoring the flush of heat rolling down my neck. "I have not seen you since I was thirteen, so it is no wonder we both look different."

Edward cocked his head to the side ever so slightly, his smile never faltering. I felt like there was something behind his eyes, but I blinked and it disappeared. Like the blood on the car door handle, it had been my imagination. Edward couldn't possibly guess that I was an imposter. Why should he? Why should anyone? The story was too far-fetched for any levelheaded person to believe.

I smiled back at the Beckinghams, confident for the first time that everything would work out. I had not been discovered, and I felt certain they did not suspect me.

4

Alice showed me to my room, making sure to point out her own room across the hall should I want to stop in for a visit later. I thanked her, promised to make time to visit soon, and closed the door, grateful for a few minutes alone.

The chauffeur had brought up my luggage and laid it at the end of the four-poster bed. Like the rest of the house, the floors in my room were cherry wood and the walls had been painted a warm cream. Maroon curtains hung from two identical windows set into the wall. They overlooked the street, and I stood in front of them, looking down at the affluent neighborhood below. The rows of town houses were well-kept. Each lawn was clipped short and flowers bloomed along the walkways. It was an entirely different world from the one I'd known in the Five Points neighborhood of New York. I'd only spent my early years there before being moved to an orphanage and then to India where I met Rose and the Beckinghams, but the memories were vivid enough to last a lifetime. The prostitutes that walked the street and men pedaling illegal or stolen goods. Everyday there was word of fights and robberies. How shocked Lord and Lady Ashton would be to know the humble beginnings of the person they had just let into their home.

While looking out on the street below, I reached into my pocket and fingered the edges of a now-worn business card. I'd read it too many times to count during the last two weeks of my sea voyage, but I pulled it from my pocket once again anyway and looked at it. The card was blank save for one name, Achilles Prideaux, and an address and telephone number.

The mysterious French gentleman had struck me as suspicious the moment I'd laid eyes on him after dinner the first night aboard the *RMS Star of* India. His thin mustache and unreadable expressions left me wary, not to mention the way he always seemed to catch me while I was alone. When Ruby Stratton's body appeared on deck, Achilles Prideaux had been one of the first people I'd suspected. However, in the end, he saved me from a most certain death at the hands of the man I'd discovered to be Ruby's murderer, Dr. Rushforth, and my opinion of Monsieur Prideaux changed forever. He disembarked at Aden, along with the bodies of Ruby Stratton and Dr. Rushforth, but before doing so, he handed me his card and told me to call on him at his London home if I ever found myself in need of his services. As I would discover later, his services included being a famous private detective.

At the time, I had considered his card to be little more than a polite gesture and had no real intention of looking him up. Now that I found myself alone in London and unable to speak to the Beckinghams about any part of my mission, however, Monsieur Prideaux seemed like a helpful ally to have. As a detective, he would be well-versed in locating and tracking down specific people—a skill that would be very useful to me in the weeks and months ahead. Plus, Rose's inheritance would ensure I had the money to hire him.

The trouble, of course, was being certain he would stop his investigation at the point I asked him to. Those who called themselves detectives were often not satisfied with half-truths or mysteries, and my story would be littered with both. I could ask him to locate the person I wanted to find, but would he then seek to uncover our connection? And if so, would that lead him to discover my true identity? If he did discover I was not always Rose Beckingham, he could feel obligated to inform the living Beckinghams, in which case, everything I'd done to get to London and get Rose's inheritance would have been for naught. Hiring Prideaux would require a great deal of caution and faith on my part, but I didn't have many other options worth considering. I decided right then that I would contact Prideaux and see if he could help me.

A knock sounded at the door and I called out that it was open. A petite woman with graying hair and a maid's uniform on slipped through the door.

"I'm here to help you dress for dinner, Miss Rose," she said, her eyes focused on the floor.

"That won't be necessary," I said, smiling, though the woman wouldn't look at my face to notice the kindness.

She shifted her weight awkwardly but didn't leave. "Lady Ashton sent me here to assist you," she clarified.

I realized then that it would be very unusual for me not to accept the maid's help. I had helped Rose dress more times than I could count and refusing assistance would cast suspicion I couldn't afford.

"Forgive me, I'm tired from my journey," I said, sinking into a low chair in the corner. "I would love your assistance."

The maid seemed visibly relieved and stepped fully into the room, closing the door behind her. I watched as she carefully unpacked my trunk, laying a green satin gown out on the bed with a lace headband and gold heels.

I stood in front of a mirror in the corner as the maid, who reluctantly told me her name was Hannah, peeled off my afternoon dress, leaving me in a corselet and my white camisole. I had a moment of panic where I worried she would notice the locket around my neck before I remembered it was no longer there.

The thought roused the memory of the two men fighting in the alley. It had been a rather exciting moment, but in all of my worries about meeting the Beckinghams and settling into my temporary home, it had slipped from my mind. I wondered whether the officer Mr. Worthing had spoken to had found the men. Or, more importantly, whether he'd found my locket. Mr. Worthing had given him my name and the address of Lord and Lady Ashton should anyone uncover it and turn it in. At the time, I was so desperate to have my locket returned I hadn't thought how dangerous that could be. What if someone did find the locket and returned it to the house? Lord and Lady Ashton would almost certainly see it and Lady Ashton, at least, would recognize that the jewelry was not nice enough to belong to a woman in Rose's position. What if she asked questions?

I took a deep breath as Hannah slipped the gown over my head. The satin breezed over my skin and I remembered where I was. *Who* I was. Or rather, who I was supposed to be. Rose would never have suffered foolish questions. If Lady Ashton did ask me about the locket, I would tell her it was a trinket I'd picked up in India and become fond of. Nothing to be ashamed of. Nothing to hide. If I walked through life on the peripheries, hiding my face, people would begin to suspect. I had to stand tall and proud.

The dinner gong sounded just as Hannah helped me slip into my shoes. She stood up, gave me a once over, and nodded her head.

"You look beautiful, Miss," she said with a smile. She had warmed to me considerably in the few minutes she'd been in my company, which was good. I needed friends. I needed people who would be on my side should my mission go south.

"Thank you, Hannah. That will be all." I offered her a smile as she left and then turned back to my reflection in the mirror.

I could not be the shy girl who had run from the dinner table aboard the ship when talk of the explosion in Simla started. I could not be the girl who hid in the shadows near the London docks while two men fought, regardless of the danger the situation presented. I needed to be a woman of action. A woman who took control of her life and her surroundings. I would start with dinner.

I adjusted the headband pressing down on my curly blonde hair and pulled my mouth into the same crooked smile Rose used to have. I was an heiress and I belonged at that table.

5

The dining room was as elegant as every other room in the house. A long wooden table filled the space, each seat set with a gold-edged plate, a crystal glass, and shiny silver utensils on a cloth napkin. It was decadent, certainly more decadent than a normal evening dinner with Rose and her family. Did the Beckinghams eat this way every night or had they deemed my return a special occasion?

I was the last to arrive at the table, and Lord Ashton and Edward rose as I entered the room. I nodded to each of them, though they seemed to be paying me as little attention as possible. They waited silently until I had sat down to reclaim their own seats. Immediately upon my arrival, Alice wanted to talk of nothing but India. The people, the clothes, the customs, the food.

"Was it warm there?" she asked, the chicken on her plate entirely forgotten. "I bet it was so warm. It never gets warm here. Did they have wonderful beaches? The beaches here are all rocks and it is too cold and dreary to swim."

"Alice, dear, finish your dinner," Lady Ashton said firmly through her smile.

Alive frowned and lowered her head.

"The coastal beaches were very nice," I said in a conspiratorial whisper, letting her know her questions were not unwelcome. "We used to enjoy them."

"We?" she asked, snapping upright.

I opened my mouth to tell her about the trips Rose and I took down to the water. About stripping off our stockings and walking in the foamy surf, about putting our sandy feet back in our shoes and running home to rinse them off. Except, I was Rose. I had to be more careful about reminiscing.

"Yes, me and my companion, Nellie," I said.

Alice turned to her mother. "A companion? Like a friend?"

"From your father's letters, I took Nellie to be your servant," Lord Ashton said.

I nodded. "You are correct, uncle. Nellie was a servant, but she was also one of my best friends."

I smiled at Alice. I didn't know why, but I felt a kinship with her. Alice was eager and excited about life, much as I had been. Rose had been the one to indulge my curiosity, and I hoped to be able to do the same for Alice.

"Did you have to pay all of your friends to spend time with you?" Edward asked. He'd spoken under his breath, but it was clear he had intended for the entire table to hear him. Catherine let out a sharp laugh, reminding me she was at the table at all. Aside from the single outburst, she hadn't made a single sound.

Lady Ashton shot her son a stern look but said nothing. Lord Ashton simply looked fatigued, as if he had long ago grown tired of Edward's behavior and no longer had the energy to correct him.

I did my best to smile, hoping if I made myself a boring target, Edward would eventually give up trying to ruffle my feathers. "We hired Nellie to assist with household chores. Luckily, she became my friend for free."

"Luckily?" Edward asked, one dark eyebrow raised. "Would you not have had the money to pay for her friendship? My understanding is that your family has enough money to make all of India your *companion*." He placed an odd emphasis on the final word.

I was startled less by his rudeness than by his frequent references to money. Although Rose and her parents had been wealthy, none of them would ever have discussed the subject so freely, and certainly not before a guest at dinner. It would not have been thought polite.

"Had, brother," Catherine said. "Her family *had* money. Unfortunately, they don't have anything anymore." Apparently, she shared her brother's ease with the topic.

I looked to Lord Ashton, expecting him to say something. Rose's father had been his brother, after all. Could he really sit by and allow his own children to speak so harshly of their deaths? Apparently, he could, as he did nothing to quiet them.

"Did you have many friends in India?" Alice asked, seeming unbothered by the antics of her older siblings.

It was a wonder she could be so well-mannered at such a young age. Perhaps, cruelty was a skill acquired with years. I hoped not. Even though I'd only just met her, I hoped Alice would stay curious and kind always.

"I did, though you'll come to find it is more important the quality of friends you surround yourself with than the quantity," I said.

"Which is lucky," Edward said, leaning forward so he could look down the table at his youngest sister. "Because we do not have the money for you to have a great quantity of friends. But we may yet be able to swing a few quality ones."

"Stop it, Edward," Alice said, hitting her hand on the table and shaking her water glass.

So, clearly Alice did understand the meanness behind her brother's words.

"It's quite all right, Alice," I said, smiling up at Edward. "What is a little teasing between cousins?"

"We have a good sport here!" Edward said, extending a hand to me as if I were livestock he was attempting to sell to an eager bidder.

Catherine snorted and swirled a pile of peas around her plate. "It's easy to be a good sport when you're the one inheriting a fortune."

"No more talk of money," Lady Ashton said. "It is impolite, particularly as dinner conversation. Dear?"

Lord Ashton nodded in agreement with his wife. "Your mother is right. Everyone ought to eat and enjoy the meal."

"While we still can," Catherine mumbled.

"Cat," Lord Ashton warned, calling her by what I assumed to be her nickname.

Lord Ashton's eldest daughter looked up at him with a meek smile and it was enough to undo the sternness in his features. He winked at her. The moment he looked away, however, Catherine cast her narrowed eyes in my direction.

What had Catherine meant by that? *While we still can.*

"You know, cousin," Edward said, speaking to me as though we were old friends. Which could have been the case. Rose had spoken to me little of her relations, so I had no idea how close she was with her family back in London. Perhaps Edward and I were meant to have been childhood friends. Based on his behavior over the course of the dinner, I found that hard to believe, but it was a possibility nonetheless.

Edward didn't seem in any particular hurry to finish his thought, so I finally looked up at him, meeting his eyes. The chandelier that hung above the table reflected in his dark irises, giving the appearance of a fire burning inside him.

"As word of the explosion in Simla reached us," Edward said, bringing up the topic as though it were as inconsequential as the weather, "we believed you to have perished in the car with your parents."

"Edward," Lady Ashton scolded, trying to pretend as though she had any control of her children. "That is hardly an appropriate topic."

"Is that true?" I asked, looking from the flushed face of my aunt to the stony face of my uncle.

I knew confirming my identity had been a point of concern. It had taken the hospital a few days to find someone who knew my family well enough to come and identify me, which was how the Worthings had been brought into the situation. They made the crucial mistake after seeing my blonde hair and clothes of deciding that I was Rose. They did not know that Rose had insisted I wear her clothes that morning. After years of me dressing her, she thought she should be allowed to dress me. She permitted me to wear one of her old chiffon dresses that had a snag in the back and a pair of black oxfords with a large scuff on the shoe.

"With my clothes on, you look like a proper lady," she'd remarked, standing back to admire her handy work.

I'd asked immediately whether I could put my own clothes back on, but Rose refused. I spent the morning feeling like a little girl playing dress up, wishing for my well-worn day dress, but I was now aware how important that series of events was in regards to my future.

I had not realized, however, that the Beckinghams ever believed me to be dead.

Lady Ashton nodded solemnly. "It was difficult to find anyone with intimate knowledge of the situation, especially in the chaotic aftermath of the attack. It took time for them to sort through the...remains of the accident, and with your injury, it made an identification difficult."

I let my hand float absentmindedly to my cheek, feeling the indentation there that would never fade.

"Yes," Edward said, drawing my attention back towards him. "We were told there had been no survivors, and after a respectable amount of mourning, we contacted our family solicitor about the matter of your inheritance."

A respectable amount? How long could that have been if they had only believed me to be dead for a couple of days? Had they cried for a few hours before turning their energy towards the thought of the fortune they would inherit?

"Of course, then we learned of your survival," Edward said, tipping his head forward, looking up at me from beneath his heavy brow. "And oh, the relief we all felt."

His words seemed kind, but I sensed a darkness in his tone. Was it sarcasm? Had Edward really wanted to say that he wished me dead?

"I'm so sorry to have put you all through so much stress. I had no idea of your troubles," I said, barely masking my anger.

I had been lying in a hospital bed, fighting for my life after surviving an attack that killed my entire family, yet Edward was concerned about the money he could have seen had I died.

Or, rather, the money he could have seen had I stayed

Nellie Dennet. Had I not assumed Rose's identity and stolen what lawfully would have been given to him. If Edward thought Rose surviving the accident was bad luck, how upset would he have been to learn Rose had died, but I'd cheated the system? A servant girl stood between him and the fortune he wanted so badly. A fortune he surely could not need anyway, given the grandness of the surroundings he already enjoyed.

"The day we learned you survived was a joyous day," Lady Ashton said. "Please, Rose, do not think any differently. Your survival lightened our despair in ways we will never be able to describe."

Alice reached out and wrapped her hand around my wrist. "You are better than a fortune," she whispered.

I turned my hand over and squeezed her fingers. "Thank you, Alice."

Lord Ashton chose not to chime in with any reassurances for me or to correct the rude behavior of his older children. Instead, he simply slid his chair away from the table, dropped his napkin in the center of his empty plate, and looked over at me. "We are happy to have you in our home, Rose. Tomorrow I will take you to the family solicitor to discuss the claiming of your inheritance."

I opened my mouth to thank him, but I was interrupted by the arrival of a butler. He wore a black suit with long coat tails and a crisp white collar. I didn't remember seeing him when I'd arrived earlier in the day, which begged the question of how many servants the Beckinghams had in their employment. However, this question faded to the back of my mind when I noted the nervous, roving eyes of the butler.

"Excuse me, Lord Ashton, but there is a police sergeant

at the door," he said. His voice was high and nasally, but he spoke in an even, measured manner.

I glanced around the table and surmised the police were not regular visitors to the Beckingham home. Lady Ashton's brows were pinned together in concern and confusion. She looked up to her husband for an answer, and he looked down at her, shrugging his shoulders.

"Did he say why he was here?" he asked.

The butler shook his head and then turned his attention to me. As he did, the rest of the family followed suit until every set of eyes in the room was on me. I flushed.

"He would like to speak to Miss Rose," the butler said, tipping his head towards me.

"Is this about the accident?" Lady Ashton asked, as if I should know.

"We will just go out there and discern what is going on," Lord Ashton said. "There's no sense sitting in here and wondering."

He walked around the table towards me and helped me scoot my chair away from the table. I stood, smoothed the wrinkles of my dress, and moved towards the door that led to the entrance hall.

"Actually," the butler said, blocking our path. "I believe the sergeant is here in connection with a recent murder."

6

Murder? My heart skipped at the word. Another murder? After the attack in Simla that had thrown my entire life into flux and the murder of Ruby Stratton on the ship from India to London, I'd assumed I had endured my fair share of murder. Was I really finding myself in the middle of another one?

"Murder?" Lady Ashton came up behind me, placing her hand on my shoulder. "Why would Rose have anything to do with a murder?"

The butler looked from Lady Ashton to Lord Ashton, his expression uncertain.

"We won't know that until we speak with the sergeant," Lord Ashton said, sounding more urgent.

"We could always ask Rose," Edward said, coming around the room until he blocked my path into the sitting room. "Who has been murdered, Rose?"

I narrowed my eyes at him. "I haven't the slightest idea."

"A murder is a pretty large thing to forget. You don't know anyone who has been murdered recently?" Edwards asked, mocking me.

He had been trying to make me look silly, but his question actually made me realize something important. "A murder occurred on the ship," I said.

Alice gasped. "Why didn't you mention that straight away?"

She was looking at me as though I'd betrayed her.

"It wasn't something I necessarily wanted to remember, and I thought the ship and local authorities were taking care of it. I spoke to several officers onboard the ship. Perhaps, they need another statement, though?"

Yes. Obviously. This had to do with Ruby Stratton. There was no other explanation.

"I'm sure that is it," Lady Ashton said.

"We won't know for sure until we get in there." Lord Ashton pushed open the door and held his hand out, directing me inside. "We shouldn't keep him waiting any longer."

We walked into the sitting room where a sergeant sat stiffly on a maroon tufted sofa. He stood as we entered.

"Good evening, Lord Ashton. Miss," he said, tipping his hat to me.

"We understand your visit is in connection with a murder?" Lord Ashton asked.

The sergeant, a mousy man with light brown hair and a round face frowned. "I'm afraid so. I hope I didn't interrupt your dinner, but we have reason to believe Miss Rose Beckingham may have been a witness to a murder."

"A witness?" I shook my head. "No, I didn't see when Ruby was murdered, but the killer did confess his crimes to me just before he attempted to kill me as well."

Confusion washed over the sergeant's face as he looked at me, mouth slightly agape. "I'm sorry, Miss. I'm not entirely sure what you are referring to."

"I'm talking about the murder of Ruby Stratton," I said.

The officer pulled out a sheet of paper and scanned it before shaking his head. "No, I'm sorry. I'm not here to discuss any Ruby Stratton. I'm here to discuss the murder of Frederick Grossmith this morning."

Lord Ashton turned to me. His broad face was darkened with suspicion. I could only imagine what he was thinking. I hadn't even been in his house one entire day and already the police were knocking on his door with talk of murder. It wasn't exactly the impression I had hoped to make.

"I don't know any Frederick Grossmith," I said. "There must be some mistake."

"You are Rose Beckingham, correct?" the sergeant asked.

I nodded. "Yes, I am."

"Did you or did you not leave your name and address with an officer near the docks this morning?"

"I did, but it was in connection with a necklace I lost," I said, trying to clarify.

"You also reported two men fighting in an alley."

My protests stilled in my throat. Of course. Yes. I had seen the two men fighting this morning. Mr. Worthing had sent an officer to investigate my claim.

The sergeant must have taken my silence as confirmation because he didn't wait for my response. "Frederick Grossmith was one of the men involved in that fight. When the officer arrived, Frederick was dead."

"Dead?" I repeated, trying to understand how that could have happened.

"Murdered," the sergeant corrected. "With a bullet that entered through his back and struck the heart."

I gasped. My vision felt blurry around the edges. He had been shot? But I'd been standing in the alley behind them. Although the fight had scared me, I had suspected the worst that would happen was they would throw a few punches and bloody one another up a bit. I never would have thought something so violent would occur.

"Here, Rose," Lord Ashton said, wrapping his hand around my upper arm and leading me to the sofa. "Sit down."

"Thank you, uncle." I let him lead me across the room, feeling suddenly faint and no longer trusting my own legs.

"I'm sorry to shock you like this, Miss, but you may very well be our only witness," the sergeant said.

"Of course, I understand," I said, practically whispering. "But I don't know how much I can tell you. I didn't see much and I left before the situation escalated."

"You said there were two men, correct? Did you get a good look at either of them?"

I squinted, trying to see back in my memory and pull every detail I could remember. "One of the men was quite a bit shorter than the other. He had dark hair and a square face. Of the two, he was definitely the most aggressive."

The sergeant wrote this down. "That sounds like Grossmith's description."

"Grossmith? The victim?" I asked.

He nodded. "What about the man he was arguing with?"

"He was in the shadows. I only saw that he was taller than Grossmith," I said.

The sergeant looked at me, eyes wide and pleading. "Do you remember *anything* else?"

I scraped my mind for anything more worth mentioning, but there was nothing. "No, I'm sorry. That is all I remember."

He pulled his lips to the side of his mouth, disappointment clear on his face. "Did you hear what they were arguing about?"

I'd heard a few words here and there, but I'd been so concerned about being caught by either man that my attention had been scattered, at best. I'd been so busy trying to get away that my brain hadn't bothered to catalog the content of the conversation. "No, I'm sorry. I don't remember anything."

"Nothing?" he pressed. "Not a single word? Grossmith was a bartender at a nearby jazz club, The Chesney Ballroom. Could the argument have had anything to do with that?"

"I'm sorry, Sergeant. I wish I could be of more help, but I didn't hear anything," I said. This was true. I wished I had more information to offer up. I didn't want a murderer roaming the streets, and if I had anything useful I would have gladly told him.

The sergeant, however, didn't seem to trust me. He narrowed his eyes and asked again. "You can't remember a single word from their conversation?"

"If my niece says she cannot remember, then she should be taken at her word," Lord Ashton said, his tone defensive and commanding. He wasn't speaking to me, and even I found myself sitting up a little straighter.

The sergeant made a note on the paper he'd brought and then stood up. "Well, I suppose that is all the questions I have for you, then, Miss Beckingham. Please let me know if you remember anything, and I will come by if I have any more questions."

"I did lose a locket necklace," I said. "It was the reason I spoke to the officer at the docks at all. I am hoping to have it returned to me. I believe I lost it near the scene of the...murder."

The officer looked at me, his expression letting me know he didn't care at all about my missing necklace. However, he still pulled out the folder he'd brought with him and checked it.

"I don't see any mention here of a necklace found at the scene of the crime, but I will be sure to keep an eye out for it," he said.

"Thank you, Sergeant."

He tipped his hat to me once again, nodded to Lord Ashton, and then wordlessly moved into the entrance hall and out the front door.

As soon as the front door shut, the door leading into the dining room blasted open and Alice shot through it, closely followed by Lady Ashton, Catherine, and Edward, who took up the rear with his arms crossed tightly over his chest, his eyes unreadable.

"You witnessed *another* murder?" Alice asked, saying it as though it were something to be proud of.

"No, I was simply near the site of a murder this morning. But so were hundreds of other people coming from the ship. I just so happened to be the person unlucky enough to see the victim before his death."

"How did he die?" she whispered, though her eyes were wide and eager.

"It's time to ready for bed, Alice," Lady Ashton said, patting her youngest daughter on the head.

"I'm not even tired," Alice protested. However, one look from her father was enough for her to press her lips tightly together and stomp up the stairs to her bedroom.

"It was nothing," Lord Ashton told the remaining members of his family. "As Rose said, she didn't see anything of import."

Lord Ashton relayed the brief interview to his wife and two eldest children while I stayed seated, trying to wrap my mind around what exactly had happened. How many police officers had I spoken to in the last five weeks? The number was surely nearing twenty.

After the attack in Simla, I had been interviewed by officers trying to find the local extremist who threw the bomb and officers who were tasked with keeping me safe until I could board the ship. Then, once I helped solve Ruby Stratton's murder, I had spoken with officers connected with the ship company and local authorities, relaying everything Dr. Rushforth had confessed and describing in detail the steps I'd taken to solve the crime before the authorities could. And now, on my first day in London, an officer had arrived during dinner to question me about yet another murder. How could one person have a front row seat to so much death and violence?

Sometime during my thoughts, Lord Ashton, Catherine, and Edward must have gone up to their rooms, because I was alone with Lady Ashton.

"Rose, dear, are you all right?" she asked, sinking down onto the seat next to me and placing her hand on my knee.

I nodded and smiled, though the effort alone made me feel weary. "Yes, I'm fine. I'm just tired from all the travel."

"I'm sure you are. I already asked Hannah to turn down your bed, so it should be ready for you."

"Thank you so much," I said. I reached out and took her hand in both of mine. "For everything. I'm so appreciative of your openness and warmth, for taking me in."

Her smile was light and airy, as if she hadn't a care in the world. It overtook her thin face in the most beautiful way. "What is family for if not to help us through our troubles?"

The fact that I was not actually Lady Ashton's family sat at the tip of my tongue, but I bit it back. We walked together upstairs, Lady Ashton keeping her arm looped through mine until we separated at the second-floor landing. She went left towards her room and I took a right.

As soon as I was alone again, my mind began trying to untangle important pieces of information from the fight I'd witnessed that morning—a distinctive article of clothing or a possible accent. Anything that would help me to assist the police in the investigation. But then, I thought about everything else I had to do. I had a meeting with the family solicitor in the morning to claim my inheritance and I needed to pay a visit to Achilles Prideaux. I had a mystery of my own to solve, and I did not have time to be solving anyone else's. From the little I'd seen of the murder victim, he didn't seem like a particularly kind man. Perhaps he deserved his death. And whether he did or did not deserve it, I didn't have any spare time to play amateur detective. It had been a fun pastime while aboard the *RMS Star of India*, where I could roam the deck and imagine myself a heroine from a novel, but other things took precedence now that I was back on land. I had to remain focused on my goal.

"You were wrong before."

I jolted at the voice, my hands coming to my heart in surprise. I hadn't seen anyone else in the hallway, and I understood that had been the intention when Edward stepped forward from the shadows. He wanted to startle me.

I composed myself as quickly as possible and squared off with him, facing him head on. "When are you referring to?" I asked at full volume. Edward wanted to hide and whisper, but I would take no part in it.

"When you first arrived, I mentioned how different you looked," Edward said, stepping closer to me. The hallway lights were dimmed, but light spilled up the stairs from the floor below, casting Edward in a ghostly glow. "You said it was probably because we had not seen one another in ten years."

I nodded. "Yes, a woman does a lot of growing in ten years. What point are you trying to make?"

Edward smiled. "My point is that you had the dates wrong. We have not seen one another in *twelve* years."

He was looking down at me with his toothy grin, and I could tell he thought he'd caught me in a trap. Edward was the only member of the family who suspected something was off about my story, and I couldn't allow him to grow more suspicious. If I allowed myself to be even slightly nervous, he would sense it. So, I laughed.

"What is two years compared to a decade?" I asked, still laughing. "Can you really fault me for rounding down?"

"Normally, no," he said, tilting his head to the side as though he were studying me. "But the two years were very important to you when you came for your last visit before leaving for India. You wrote me while I was at school, lamenting how long it had been since you'd last seen me. I am only surprised you have forgotten your anguish so quickly."

"Ten years is not so quick," I said.

He pursed his lips. "I suppose you are right. Time does make strangers of us all. Hopefully we will be as close as we once were."

I reached out, closing the distance between us, and laid my hand on his shoulder. Edward visibly flinched as we touched but did not move away. "I'm sure we will, cousin."

We stared at one another for a moment, and I sensed we were vying for power, each pulling on the end of a long rope, trying to topple the other over. In the end, Edward looked away first. He stepped away from my hand and turned towards the stairs. His room was on the first floor, putting a distance between us I was grateful for.

"Goodnight, Rose," he said over his shoulder, not bothering to turn around. "I hope you'll sleep well."

I gladly closed myself in my bedroom and sank back against the thick wooden door. Was Edward simply trying to unbalance me or did he truly have suspicions I was not who I claimed to be? I knew he wanted my inheritance, but would his desire for the money be enough for him to try and create doubt about my identity?

Surely not.

Or at least, I hoped not.

I prepared for bed, worrying constantly of what would become of me and my plan should my identity be revealed. After tossing and turning for nearly an hour, I fell into a fitful sleep, dreaming of Edward's smile, his face twisting and turning until I was looking down at Frederick Grossmith.

7

I walked into the family solicitor's office mid-morning. Lord Ashton held the door open for me, and I stepped inside, followed by Lady Ashton. Edward had asked to join us, but his father had put a stop to the idea. I had not been privy to the full conversation, but their whispered tones had found me as I was standing in the entrance hall to the house, and it sounded heated. I suspected it had something to do with Edward's behavior at dinner the night before. Lord Ashton may not have reprimanded his adult son for acting like a child in their home, but he would not allow himself or his family to be embarrassed while in public. So, thankfully, I was accompanied only by my aunt and uncle.

The office was run-down, but clean. Paint was chipping off the walls in the waiting room and the stain on the receptionist's desk had long ago begun to fade. The wood floors were heavily worn where foot traffic was heaviest, and the solicitor's name—Wilfred Barnett—was stenciled onto a fading wooden sign that hung predominantly in the lobby.

"Are you nervous?" Lady Ashton asked. "Because there is

no reason to be nervous. None at all. This is just a meeting to sign paperwork and discuss the next steps."

"No, I'm fine," I said truthfully. If Edward had joined us, I would have been concerned about what he may or may not have had hiding up his sleeve, but I trusted my aunt and uncle to see my inheritance given to me without a fight.

"Good, good," Lady Ashton said, her breathing slightly erratic. "Because Mr. Barnett is a good man. Lawyers receive a bad reputation, but they are people just like the rest of us."

"I don't know if I'd go that far. Have you ever had dinner with a lawyer?" Lord Ashton laughed and then turned to his wife. "Dear, your fidgeting is enough to make anyone nervous."

Lady Ashton's foot had been shaking since the moment we'd sat down. I didn't know her well enough yet to be familiar with her usual countenance, but she did seem slightly more anxious than she had the day before.

"I'm sorry," she said. "All this official business makes me nervous. I wish we could handle family affairs without the help of strangers."

"Can you imagine the chaos that would ensue if there was no legal documentation?" Lord Ashton asked, incredulous. "Brother would kill brother for the chance at a fortune."

Lady Ashton gasped. "Surely you don't mean that, dear."

"I do not mean myself," he said. "But there are many families less loving than ours who would do anything to get rich quick."

I had to wonder whether Lord Ashton was thinking of his own son in the same way I was. If it weren't for Wilfred Barnett, I suspected Edward would have betrayed just about anyone to get his hands on the Beckingham fortune.

"Miss Rose Beckingham?" The receptionist stood up

from behind her desk and smiled at me. Her brown hair fell in loose waves down to her shoulders, and she wore a starched gray dress that gave her a slim, boxy shape, pairing it with a cream white sweater partly buttoned. "Mr. Barnett is ready for you."

She led us into an office that was nearly the same size as the waiting room. Bookshelves lined the two side walls, filled from floor to ceiling with large leather volumes and bronze busts of various men throughout history. Wilfred Barnett sat behind his desk, looking wide and important, his hands folded in front of him.

"Welcome, welcome. Come in, come in," he said, repeating everything twice.

"Thank you, thank you," I said, unable to help myself as I took one of the wooden chairs across from his desk. Lord and Lady Ashton sat on either side of me.

"I understand we are here about the subject of Miss Beckingham's inheritance?" Mr. Barnett asked, licking his thumb and flipping through a pile of papers on his desk.

"Yes, that is correct," Lord Ashton said.

As he flipped through the documents, Wilfred's eyebrows rose. "I thought you were dead," he said, looking up at me.

I smiled, but Mr. Barnett continued to stare at me, and I understood he wanted me to make some form of response. I stumbled. "Um...well...I'm not," was the best I could manage.

"Clearly," he said, nodding and returning his focus to the documents before him.

"Now, the good news is that you are alive and very capable of claiming your inheritance."

"Yes, that is good news," I said, resisting the temptation to roll my eyes.

"The bad news," he continued, "is that, according to these documents, you are unmarried?"

Lord Ashton shifted in his chair next to me.

"Correct. I am not married."

Mr. Barnett puckered his lips and shook his head, disappointed. "You will be unable to claim the full breadth of your family's fortune until you are married."

It felt as though someone were squeezing my chest, forcing the breath from my lungs. "What?" I gasped, trying to be certain Mr. Barnett had actually said what I thought he'd said.

He skimmed over the documents once more quickly, laid them down, and then looked at me, his hands folded over the pages in front of him. "Yes, I'm afraid your father's will contains a rather old fashioned stipulation that you must be married to claim your inheritance. Until then, you will be offered a monthly allowance that will cover your basic needs and expenses."

"This is nonsense," I said, sitting forward and reaching for the papers.

"Now, Rose," Lady Ashton said, reaching for my arm.

I shook her off. "Why would he do something like this?"

"You'll find it is actually quite common—or it used to be in the old days," Mr. Barnett said.

Lord Ashton hummed in agreement. "Fathers want their daughters to marry and carry on the bloodline, Rose, especially when there is a family fortune at stake and only one heir to inherit."

I looked at him, mouth open. "If Catherine were to find herself a spinster, would you wish to condemn her further by ensuring she remain a poor one? That does not seem like a father's love in action to me."

Lord Ashton's face went red, but just as he opened his

mouth, Lady Ashton stood up and grabbed my shoulder. "You are upset, Rose. We understand. But I am afraid there is nothing we can do on the matter. The only person who could change the will has died. As it is, you will receive your allowance until you are married. And that shall be the end of it."

I wanted to argue, but I could see it would do no good. Lady Ashton was right. No one there could help me, and when Mr. Barnett revealed what my monthly allowance would be, I realized things were not quite as dire as they had seemed. Though the stipulation that I marry to receive my money was antiquated, I could live quite well on the money I would be allowed. Growing up poor had made me more than capable of managing my money, a skill most women inheriting their family's fortunes did not have.

By the time we left the office, having signed all the necessary forms and made arrangements for my allowance to be delivered to Ashton House until further notice, Lord Ashton's temper had cooled considerably.

"You are more than welcome to make your home with us, Rose," Lord Ashton said, looking straight ahead as he spoke, rather than making eye contact with me.

"Yes," Lady Ashton said, shaking her head so hard I thought it would fall off and roll across the wooden floor. "We would love to have you as long as you would like."

I smiled at them both in thanks. Though I had grown quite fond of the couple in the two days I'd known them, I knew I wouldn't be able to remain living with them. The first issue was that, no matter how good my deception was, they were not actually my relatives. Time would certainly make me complacent and the more time I spent with the London Beckinghams, the more time they would have to ascertain that I did not know as much about their family or my past as I should. It would be better for me to make my home elsewhere and visit them frequently. Especially with Edward nosing around, trying to trip me up at every turn. So far, I had been able to brush away his questions and doubts easily enough, but my constant presence would only make him more persistent in finding some reason why he should be the inheritor of my money.

As we left the solicitor's office, I was struck by how much warmer the day had become. The sun had decided to make a rare appearance from behind the slate gray clouds and I looked up, eyes closed, trying to soak in the warmth before it disappeared. I must have found the warmth a bit too comforting, because my breathing deepened and my body relaxed enough that my purse dropped from my hands and fell onto the cement.

"No worries, Miss Rose, I will get that for you." The chauffeur, George, was coming around the front of the car to open the door for me. He had sped up as he noticed me stooping to pick up my purse.

Usually, I would have assured him I was capable of doing it myself, but I knew it would raise the suspicions of the Beckinghams, so I simply stood back and allowed George to return my purse to me.

He never met my eyes as he stooped down and handed me my bag, and as he reached out to open the door for me, I noticed the tremble in his hands. He wore thick driving gloves. The leather was a rich brown color with tan stitching, and they looked to be quite expensive. I wondered whether the Beckinghams supplied his driving gloves or whether he had purchased them himself.

I followed Lord and Lady Ashton into the car and smiled at George through the window as he closed the door. He pulled his lips into a nervous twitch that could techni-

cally be classified as a smile, and then walked around
the car.

As we moved through London, back to the Beckingham
home, I couldn't stop thinking on George's gloves. Certainly,
all chauffeurs wore driving gloves of some kind. At least,
chauffeurs of respectable families probably did. So why was
I so fixated on George's gloves? It wasn't until we were home
and I was climbing out of the car, George dutifully holding
the door open for me, that I thought back to the previous
morning. To the smear of blood on the door handle and
George's bare hands.

I hadn't noticed the gloves the previous morning
because he hadn't been wearing them. That alone was no
cause for alarm, but it made me wonder whether the blood
I'd seen on the door handle had truly been my overactive
imagination, as I'd thought at the time, or whether it had
actually been there. George had been late to pick me up and
he'd been in the area where the fight and murder occurred.
Could he have killed Frederick for reasons unknown and
then hurried to drive me to Ashton House, stuffing his
bloodied gloves in his pocket to clean later?

I shook my head, trying to dispel the thin theory. It was
ridiculous. For one thing, the victim had been shot, presumably from some distance, making it unlikely that blood
would have gotten onto the hands of his killer. Anyway, I
was seeing clues where there were none to be found. It was
likely not required for George to wear his gloves all the time,
so it shouldn't be unusual for him to be seen barehanded.
And making the leap from missing gloves to committing a
murder was quite extreme. It was more likely that in his
haste to hurry and pick me up, he had forgotten his gloves.
After all, people who are late are significantly more likely to
be moving in a hurry and forget things.

"Thank you, George," Lady Ashton said as she slipped out of the car and straightened her bucket hat on her hat.

George tipped his hat to his employer, bending forward to reveal the top of his auburn head.

"Yes, thank you, George," I said, smiling at him.

George tipped his hat to me much less eagerly than he had to Lady Ashton, and when his eyes finally did meet mine, he cast them quickly back to the ground.

Someone so nervous could never be a murderer, I thought to myself. However, wouldn't someone who had committed a murder have good reason to be nervous?

My mind went on like that, debating back and forth the likelihood of George the chauffeur being a murderer, until I met Lady Ashton and Catherine for mid-afternoon tea.

8

Catherine arrived to tea a few minutes after I did, looking radiant. She had changed into a shimmering tea gown that cut off mid-calf and floated weightlessly around her body. She paired the ensemble with a silver headband around her blonde hair and a long string of pearls.

"You look like one of those flapper girls," Lady Ashton said, though her tone hinted that she did not deem 'flapper' to be a compliment.

"Thank you, mother," Catherine said with a wicked smile, taking her seat.

I hadn't bothered to change out of the pale pink dress I'd slipped on that morning, which did not go unnoticed by Catherine.

"Were you not aware we always have afternoon tea?" she asked, eying my ensemble up and down, a sneer on her face.

"I was quite aware," I said, smiling. "I simply forgot how often women in London change their clothes."

The sentence was unassuming enough, but I knew Catherine understood the criticism I'd laced through each word. She was a woman who knew how to smile and laugh all the while planning to plunge her dessert fork into your back. Two could play that game.

The conversation quickly shifted to more banal topics. Lady Ashton spoke of her friends and their children, giving a large amount of attention to the eldest sons.

"Did you know Hugh Anderson is studying to become a doctor?" she asked, nudging her daughter, eyebrows raised. "He is quite handsome."

"You think every man is quite handsome," Catherine said. "Especially if his dead relatives leave him comfortably situated."

Lady Ashton reared back as though she'd been slapped. "You make me out to be a snob, Cat. Do you think so little of your mother?"

Catherine smiled, not at all put off by her mother's hurt feelings. "No. In fact, I think highly enough of you to know you are a master manipulator. You want to guilt me out of my opinion, but it cannot be done. I formed my view of you long ago, and little can be done to sway me."

Lady Ashton took a sip of her tea, but it appeared she only did so to try and hide her smile. It was a wonder to me that two women, regardless of their familial connection, as different as Lady Ashton and Catherine could ever get along. Yet, they carried the conversation through the first two cups of tea and the first plate of scones while I sat back and listened. I had never been permitted to take tea with Rose in India, though I had often sat quietly in the corner should she need anything. The view from the table was much different than the one from the corner.

"I shouldn't eat another bite," Lady Ashton said as a silver tray of tarts were brought out and set in the center of the table. Despite her words, she reached for a berry tart and took a dainty bite, groaning in pleasure as it passed her lips.

"We ought to hire a less accomplished cook," Catherine said. "I will need a new wardrobe if the desserts continue to be this delicious."

Then, both women looked over at me. Clearly, it was my turn to compliment the food. That was difficult, however, seeing as I hadn't eaten anything in the last twenty minutes.

"Rose, are you not going to have *any* of the tarts?" Lady Ashton asked.

I placed a hand on my stomach and shook my head. "I am beyond full from the scones. They were delicious, though, so I suspect the tarts are equally as good."

"They are better," Catherine said, picking one up and handing it to me. My first instinct was to pull away from her, certain she must have poisoned it, but she seemed to be experiencing a moment of genuine kindness. Her eyes were bright and kind. For the first time, I realized she had Lady Ashton's eyes.

"I really couldn't," I insisted, waving her away.

Catherine tilted her head to the side, her eyebrows pulled together in the center. "You used to have such a sweet tooth. We couldn't have baked enough desserts in the world to satisfy you."

"Yes, I thought raspberry tarts were your favorite," Lady Ashton said. "I had them made for you specifically."

A jolt of panic raced through me, but I took a steadying breath and composed myself. "I've done my best over the years to curb my natural tendency towards desserts, but if you both insist, I will indulge."

I took the tart from Catherine and bit into it, doing my best not to wince at the sweetness. Rose had always preferred sweet desserts much more than I did. When I did eat a tart, I preferred the natural bite of citrus and herb over the syrupy sweetness of a berry.

Lady Ashton looked at me expectantly as I chewed and swallowed. "Delicious," I said, smiling and assuring her I enjoyed it. At their insistence, I ate two more tarts before finally excusing myself.

I moved lethargically up the stairs to my room, feeling as though I could be sick on the stairs. It had been a long time since I'd eaten so many servings of a dessert, and I hoped I wouldn't be forced to do it again anytime soon.

I pushed open the door to my room, but it hit something and came bouncing back towards me. I yelped and threw out my hands to stop it.

"Sorry, sorry," a small voice squeaked.

Alice came out from behind the door, her hands raised in apology, cheeks flushed with embarrassment.

"Alice?" I asked, moving into the room and pushing the door closed behind me. "What are you doing in here?"

The lid to my steamer trunk was thrown back and the things I hadn't yet unpacked were scattered around the floor in stacks. I looked from the mess to Alice and back again. Was she spying on me? Had Edward sent her to snoop through my room in search of evidence I wasn't who I claimed to be? I had no such evidence hidden in my room, but still the thought made my blood boil.

"I should have asked," Alice said, lowering her face and throwing her hands over her eyes. "Tea was taking so long and I grew bored. I'm sorry."

I shook my head, trying to push down my anger until I had a proper explanation for Alice's actions. "You aren't making any sense. Why are you going through my things?"

"I thought perhaps you may have brought something interesting back with you from India." She looked up at me through her long eyelashes. Her features were pulled down into a forced frown, but her eyes were still bright with excitement.

I wanted to condemn her for going through my things without permission, but the thought of upsetting the person who liked me best in the entire house seemed too bleak to consider, so I smiled and lowered myself to the floor. I crossed my legs and resituated my dress over my knees.

"I'm sure you didn't find anything very exciting," I admitted, picking up a white embroidered cloche hat and setting it in my lap.

She nodded, the disappointment clear on her face.

"Sorry," I said, tossing her my hat. She caught it just before it could land in her lap and quickly pulled it on. It fell over her eyes so she had to tilt her head back to see me. "I wasn't able to pack very much before moving back here. All of my souvenirs were left behind."

She grew somber. "Of course, I didn't think of that."

"That's all right," I said, dipping low to catch her eyes and smiling.

Alice stood up and made to leave. "I should leave you alone. My mother told me I should be sure to give you your space."

I grabbed her hand before she could go. "I insist you stay. We could do something fun."

"Like what?" Alice asked, immediately falling back to the floor, looking at me eagerly.

"We could play a game?"

She nodded, her brown hair falling around her face.

"Ask me any strange question you can think of and I'll answer it," I said.

Alice immediately screwed up her face in concentration. When she thought of a question, she rose up to her knees, hand held up in the air as though she'd just had a genius idea. "Have you ever been kissed before?"

"Alice!"

She smiled and crossed her arms. "You have to answer the question. It's part of the game."

I narrowed my eyes at her playfully. I had kissed a servant boy the Beckinghams employed when I was only fifteen-years-old. He snuck me flowers from the front garden and Rose teased me mercilessly after I confided how handsome I thought he was. But I couldn't very well tell that story to Alice. Rose would never have kissed a servant boy. Even if she was friends with me, she still had standards, especially when it came to men. To my knowledge, though, she had never kissed anyone. And if she had, she hadn't told me about it.

"I have never kissed anyone," I said.

"Liar!"

"Why would I lie about something like that?" I asked.

"You're beautiful and you were in India. It's exotic and warm. Surely, the men swarmed around you," Alice said, her eyes dreamy.

"I think your image of India is too picturesque. It was so hot that several months of every year were dedicated to sweating. No men wanted to be around me during that time."

Alice shook her head. "I can't believe it. I was sure you would have kissed someone before."

"Sorry to disappoint you," I said. "But now it is my turn."

Alice sat down and rubbed her hands together nervously.

That simple action brought to mind the chauffeur again. I had forgotten about him over mid-afternoon tea, but now he was front and center in my mind.

"Where does the chauffer sleep?" I asked, almost absent-mindedly.

"George Hoskins?" Alice asked, her face screwed up in confusion.

I nodded.

"That's a boring question. Ask me another," she said.

"It's my question," I laughed. "You have to answer it."

"All of the servants have rooms in the attic," she said.

I felt a chill threaten to run down my spine. George lived in this house? What if, by some wild chance, he was a murderer? How would I be able to sleep knowing he was only one floor above me?

"But," Alice continued, "George sleeps in the carriage house around back."

"Carriage house?" I asked. "The family has carriages in 1926?"

"It's only called the carriage house. It was converted into a garage for the cars several years ago," she explained.

"Then George lives in the garage?" I asked, still confused.

Alice rolled her eyes, exasperated. "No, Rose. He lives in a room attached to the garage. We wouldn't house someone in the garage, for goodness sake."

The game continued on for a few more minutes, but Alice quickly became bored with my questions and she left to ready herself for dinner. In her absence, I finally had a second to think on the information I'd gathered.

Although I felt reasonably confident my suspicions about George being involved in the murder of Frederick Grossmith were just that—suspicions—I still felt like I needed to more thoroughly look into him as a serious suspect. I had already decided that it was not the time nor place to get involved with another murder investigation, but that was before someone within the Beckingham household had arisen as a person of interest. I couldn't very well live in close proximity to a man who had possibly committed a murder without looking into it. Or perhaps leaving the matter alone would be the right thing to do. I fell back on my bed, riddled with indecision.

Then, the answer came to me. My own troubles were holding me back from investigating this most recent murder, so perhaps the solution would be to seek out the famous detective, Achilles Prideaux. I could ask him about assisting me in my search, and depending on his answer, I would know whether I had the time and opportunity to look into Frederick's murder.

Yes, that was the solution. It was time to call upon Monsieur Prideaux.

9

I rose before the sun the next morning and dressed as quietly as I could. I opted for a midnight blue pleated skirt, pale blue blouse, and a cream cardigan buttoned over the top to keep out the early morning chill.

As I tip-toed through the house, I didn't hear another sound. All of the lights were still off, and even the kitchen, which was usually buzzing with maids and cooks, was silent. I slipped through the front door and into the foggy London morning.

The street the Beckinghams lived on was desolate, so I had to walk several blocks before I was able to flag down a cab. The driver gave me a curious look as I climbed into the backseat, but he was in no mood to turn down money. I handed him Monsieur Prideaux's business card and directed him to take me to the address on the card. He nodded and pulled away without further question.

The cab pulled up in front of a long row of brick buildings that spanned the whole block. Each was four-stories tall with a large black roof that sat atop it like a straw hat.

"Do you want me to wait for you?" the driver asked as he handed me back the business card.

"If you would," I said. I wasn't sure how long my conversation with Achilles would take or if he was even home. I didn't want to have to go to the trouble of finding another cab so early in the morning.

The driver agreed and leaned back in his seat, pulling his hat down over his eyes to, presumably, take a quick nap.

I walked down the street, reading the wooden signs affixed to the buildings until I came to 'Building 300.' The card listed Achilles' flat number as 301 A, which was on the first floor. I mounted a short set of stone steps and knocked three times.

It was early, but not early enough that calling upon an old friend would be seen as suspicious. Achilles and I weren't exactly old friends, of course, but he was the closest thing I had to a friend in London. I didn't know anyone there aside from the Beckinghams.

After a minute or two with no answer, I knocked again, slightly harder than the first time. Part of me felt bad for potentially waking him up, but a larger part of me wished to speak to him and didn't want to come back later. While I waited, I double-checked the business card to be sure I was at the right address.

"Are you here for Monsieur Prideaux?" a female voice asked.

I looked around, trying to discern where the voice had come from.

A whistle came from above me and I looked up to find a gray-haired woman sticking halfway out of the window directly above Achilles Prideaux's door.

I stepped back so I didn't have to strain my neck so much

to see her. "Yes, I'm here for Monsieur Prideaux. He gave me his business card while we were—"

"He isn't home," she said, cutting me off.

"Oh." My disappointment was obvious. "Do you know where he is?"

She waved her hand and rolled her eyes. "Probably off to some corner of the globe or other solving the murder of a duchess or hunting down a jewel thief. The last postcard he sent came from someplace called Aden."

The port of Aden was where Achilles Prideaux had left the *RMS Star of India*. I'd assumed he was stopping off briefly to assist in closing the case of Ruby Stratton's murder and Dr. Rushforth's suicide and would soon continue his journey aboard a different ship, but there was no way to know for sure.

"Did he say when he would be back?" I asked.

The woman held up one finger and disappeared back inside. She was gone for several minutes, long enough that I questioned whether I should leave or not, and then she reappeared.

"His postcard was recent. I would guess he will be back sometime in the next few days. I can't say how long he'll stay, though. He travels frequently."

"How do you know Monsieur Prideaux?" I wanted to know how credible her information was.

"I own the building," she said. "He's my favorite tenant. He always pays on time and he's never here."

With that, the woman closed the window and drew the curtains closed.

I turned back to the street where the cab driver was waiting. I'd snuck out with the intention of speaking to Monsieur Prideaux, but I had other plans, as well. Not all was lost. I climbed back into the cab, woke the driver, and gave him my destination.

"A cemetery?" he asked, merging with the early morning traffic.

I simply nodded and sat back in the seat, watching as the sunrise painted the sky in a wash of pastel pinks and yellows.

By the time we reached the cemetery, the sun was fully over the horizon, highlighting the dew drops on every blade of grass, turning the cemetery into a field of silver. Lady Ashton had told me about the stone marker she had dedicated to Rose's parents, and immediately I knew I would have to visit. I'd been rushed out of India before I could attend any sort of memorial service for the family, and the explosion had made it impossible to send their remains back to London for a burial. So, the memorial stone would have to do.

"Shall I wait again?" the driver asked, prepared to sink down into the seat and wait for me.

I shook my head. "Home isn't far from here. I'll walk. Thank you."

I handed him the money and a generous tip and waited until he disappeared down the street before stepping through the iron gates of the cemetery. I wove through cracked headstones and decaying flowers until I came to a freshly tilled plot of earth.

The stone was crisp and gray, standing out from the weather-worn, dull stones that surrounded it. Etched into the stone were each of their names, the letters deeply carved and painted black. William Alexander Beckingham and Elizabeth Rose Beckingham.

I bent down and ran a finger over the stone, tracing their

names and whispering them into the morning air. Lady Ashton had offered to accompany me to the cemetery, but it was a trip I needed to make alone. I needed to make my peace with the people who had given me a home. I had worked for the family as a servant, but they had saved me from an orphan's life. They had given me a companion in Rose, and now, they had given me a chance. A chance to right the wrongs of my past. I could never properly thank them for that if Lady Ashton was around.

"I'm sorry Rose's name isn't next to yours," I whispered. "I wish she could be here with you. I wish everyone who came to visit you would think of Rose and remember what a wonderful person she was."

My words grew thick with unshed tears, but I pushed on. I needed to say what was on my mind. "I will always remember her, though. I know that may not be worth much to you, but it is all I can offer. And Rose, I know you are here, too, if only in spirit. I want to thank you for what you've given me. For lending me your clothes and allowing me to take the window seat that day in the car. You saved my life. I wish I could trade places with you, but since I can't, I'm trying to do the most I can with the life I have been given. I know you would understand, and I hope you are proud."

A wind blew through the cemetery, lifting my short-cropped hair, and it felt like a sign. It probably wasn't, but I was desperate for something, anything that would make me feel better about the choices I had made since the deaths of Rose and her family. Being the only person in the world to know of Rose's death was a dreadfully heavy weight to carry around. Over the years we lived together in India, Rose had become a dear friend, and now there was no one with whom I could mourn her loss. I was riddled with guilt and grief, so I would accept even a random gust of wind if it would help lighten my load.

"I knew you would understand, Rose," I said, beginning to feel foolish for spending so long talking to myself in a graveyard. "I miss you."

I slipped from the graveyard quietly and began moving down the sidewalk in the direction of Ashton House. The sky had lightened considerably and the sounds of the day beginning were all around me. Cars rumbled down the road and voices drifted from the open windows of the houses that lined the streets. Large Elm trees hung overhead, creating an intricate web of light and dark on the ground.

The weight of the cemetery was already washing off of me. I hadn't been able to meet with Achilles Prideaux like I'd wanted, but I was hopeful I'd speak with him soon. In the meantime, I planned to take in as much of London as I could and try to focus on having a normal life. The explosion had turned everything upside down, and what I need more than anything else was some stability. I needed some time to take a few deep breaths and relax.

As I turned onto the Beckingham's road, a group of people up ahead caught my eye. The bright morning sun cast the group in silhouette, so I couldn't see exactly what was happening, but whatever it was, it seemed exciting. As I walked closer, I could begin to make out the conversation.

"You said you met her aboard the ship?" a male voiced asked gruffly.

"Yes, she gave me this card." The smaller figure held out a thin arm and handed something off to the couple in front of him. It was then that I recognized the boy's voice and was able to place the man's.

My aunt and uncle were standing on the street speaking with Aseem, the Indian stowaway I'd befriended aboard the *RMS Star of India*. He'd assisted me with my investigation into Ruby Stratton's murder, and had wormed his way into my heart. Shortly before disembarking in London, I'd sought out the boy, handed Aseem the Beckingham's address, and told him to seek me out should he find himself in any trouble. Apparently, his plans had fallen through and he was in need of my assistance.

I sped up, moving as quickly down the street as I could, and Lady Ashton looked over as I neared them, relief coloring her face. From her dress, I sensed she and Lord Ashton must have been out and had encountered Aseem in front of the house just as they were returning home again.

"Oh, Rose, thank goodness," she said, brushing past a nervous looking Aseem and her husband to extend an arm out to me. "You can help us settle this."

"This young boy claims to know you," Lord Ashton said, hitching a thumb towards Aseem who cast his wide brown eyes up at me.

"Yes, we met on the ship," I said, looking from my aunt to my uncle and then smiling down at Aseem. "How have you been?"

He nodded, his face serious for such a young boy. "I've been better and worse. I'm glad to have found you, though."

"You gave him our address?" Lord Ashton asked, eyebrow raised. It was clear he didn't approve of the gesture, but I couldn't very well let a young boy wander into a new city alone with no one to turn to for help.

"He assisted me with a...project while we were on the ship," I said, breezing past the fact that Aseem used his ability to move undetected to spy for me. "I only wanted to extend the same courtesy and assist him should he need it."

Lady Ashton smiled. "That is lovely, Rose. You always were so good at making friends in unexpected places."

"Unexpected, indeed," Lord Ashton mumbled under his breath.

"Do you think I could speak to Aseem alone for a moment?" I asked.

Lord Ashton seemed ready to fight me on it, but Lady Ashton looped her arm through his and meandered down the block just out of earshot.

"You found me rather quickly, Aseem," I said, the words both a statement and a question.

He smiled apologetically and tipped his head to the side. "Yes, things did not go as I expected them to. I was supposed to meet someone, but they haven't appeared, and I'm afraid I have nowhere else to go."

"What exactly are you hoping I can do for you?" I asked. Without the full amount of my inheritance, my options were limited. I would have loved to be able to promise him shelter and maybe a position as a servant in my own house, but it would be some time before I could move out of Ashton House. Aseem might very well starve by then.

"Food and shelter are what I need most," he said, looking behind me to where Lord and Lady Ashton were standing beneath the shade of an Elm, having what appeared to be a heated conversation. "But I understand if that is not possible."

I bit my lip. "Yes, that could be difficult. I do not have a home of my own, otherwise I would gladly offer you a place to stay."

"I understand," Aseem said, taking a step back and preparing to turn and leave. "I do not wish to trouble you."

"Don't go anywhere just yet," I said, holding out a hand to stop him. "Let me speak with my aunt and uncle. I'm sure they would be glad to help you."

Aseem nodded, but I could see the doubt in his eyes. Lord Ashton was a hard man, not nearly as kind as his wife, and it was clear he intimidated Aseem. I smiled at him, trying to offer some reassurance, and then went to speak to the Beckinghams.

"You really know that child?" Lord Ashton asked, narrowing his eyes at me.

"He's a good boy," I said, sensing the words my uncle was leaving unspoken. It was clear he did not trust Aseem, despite not knowing him in the slightest. "He is all alone in the city."

Lady Ashton placed a hand over her heart. "Alone?" she repeated, her lower lip puckered out.

"He travelled here from India just as I did, but the person he was supposed to meet did not show. He has no one to turn to."

Lord Ashton looked unmoved, but Lady Ashton turned to her husband, her face a mask of pitiful sorrow. "We have to help him, James."

He shook his head. "No, we do not, *Eleanor*."

"He is not asking for charity. He will work for his supper. I'm sure he would just be glad for a warm bed," I said.

"We have enough help as it is," Lord Ashton said. "Perhaps, if we had an open position I would rethink—"

"It wouldn't be permanent," I said, interrupting him. "Once I have a place of my own, I will hire him as my own personal errand boy."

"A place of your own?" Lady Ashton asked, her expression dripping with despair for another reason now.

I reached out and wrapped a hand around her wrist, smiling at her. "Not immediately, dear aunt. But eventually, yes. I do not want to overstay my welcome."

Lady Ashton gave me a sad smile and then turned to her husband. "Do you wish to cost our niece a trusted servant? If we do not hire him, he will find work elsewhere and she will never forgive us."

"I would forgive—" I started to say but stopped when Lady Ashton cast a narrow-eyed warning my way.

She then turned her attention back to her husband. "He looks like a healthy, capable boy. Surely there is something he can help with."

Lord Ashton's face remained immovable, but his posture altered slowly from one of rigidity to a slouched, tired stance. It was clear he had waged too many battles with his wife to have any hope of winning this one. After a few seconds, he nodded, waved a hand as if to dismiss us both, and stomped up the cement walkway towards the house.

"He puts on a show but he has a soft heart underneath it all," Lady Ashton said, a conspiratorial smile on her lips.

When I relayed the good news to Aseem, he thanked me repeatedly, insisting he would be nothing but loyal to me and my family.

"How can I help you?" he asked eagerly, bouncing back and forth on his threadbare shoes.

I smiled down at him and placed a hand on his shoulder. "Today, I need you to settle into your new room, take a bath, and get some rest. I'll have breakfast sent up in half an hour."

Aseem lunged out and wrapped his arms around me. It was an odd show of emotion from the boy. He had acted well beyond his years since the moment I'd met him, but it was clear to me now how desperate he'd been for my help. When he pulled away from me, he straightened his stained tunic and beamed up at me, brown eyes wide and glimmering.

10

The garden in front of the Beckingham's house was well-kept, but the noise from the street made it difficult to relax there. Not to mention, Edward's bedroom window looked out on the front of the house, and he apparently found it quite enjoyable to watch me amble around the garden. He wouldn't even try to hide himself. He would pull the curtains back and stand in full view so I would know he was watching me. Given his rather ominous presence, I'd taken to circling the back garden several times a day. After first disembarking the ship, I thought I'd miss the dry heat of India forever, but the cool, damp London air was beginning to grow on me.

A well-trodden path ran around the edge of the garden, along the wrought iron fence woven with yellow bursts of sweet-smelling honeysuckle. When I felt certain no one was looking, I would pluck a handful of honeysuckle from the plant and suck the nectar from the ends. That was what I was doing when I saw the chauffeur, George, shut the door to his room, which was connected to the garage, and then move around the back of the building. I pushed myself into the climbing flowers, even though I had every right to be in the back garden and didn't actually need to hide. A few seconds later, the car roared to life and George reversed out of the garage and took off down the alley.

Until that moment, I'd been doing my best to keep my mind on other matters. Which hadn't been exactly difficult. Since moving to London, I'd had a lot to contend with, and the murder of a stranger wasn't particularly high on the list. However, the more I interacted with George, the more I began to wonder whether he wasn't the man I'd seen in the alley with the murder victim. At just over six feet tall, he was the right height, and the man I'd seen wore a similar suit and hat to George, though it was a common look and many men certainly dressed similarly. Still, try as I might, I couldn't rule him out as a suspect. But here was my chance. His room was empty, and no one would know if I just snuck in, took a look around, and left quietly. It would put my mind at ease and help me to forget about Frederick Grossmith.

I ambled along the fence as casually as I could, simultaneously keeping an eye out for anyone who could be watching me. Satisfied I was perfectly alone, I ventured off the path, cutting across the manicured lawn to George's door. It was unlocked, and I quickly stepped inside.

The space was dark and cold. Alice had told me the entire building had once been used as a carriage house, and I could tell. Beneath a thin carpet, the floor was cold stone. Large, drafty windows replaced what was once the door for the carriages to come in and out of.

Still, despite the circumstances, George had made his area homey. He had a winged armchair with a fringed reading lamp next to it. Shelves full of books filled a small nook next to a modest closet, and his bed was tucked away in a back corner, the sheets meticulously creased and wrapped under the mattress. The neatness of his space surprised me, not only because he was a man, and in my experience, men were rarely tidy, especially when living alone. But also because the neatness of the room stood in stark contrast to the small metal garbage can sitting in a corner of the room, black smoke swirling out of it.

I grabbed a throw blanket from the back of the chair and ran across the room, prepared to smother the flames, but there was no need. The fire had burnt itself out—rather recently, I noted—leaving behind a pile of ash and cinders.

I reached for the garbage can, but it was still much too hot to touch and I yanked back my hand, plunging my pointer finger into my mouth to soothe it. The smoke was still spilling out in thick clouds, but George wouldn't have lit a fire in his room for no reason. Clearly, he'd been trying to destroy something, and I needed to know what. I fanned the smoke away, the rush of air flickering an ember in the bottom of the can. That tiny ember illuminated enough for me to see something that wasn't ashes or cinder. It was solid and thick.

George had a small kitchen sink in a corner of the room with a shelf above it containing a few dishes and, at the end, a stack of dish towels. I grabbed one and wrapped it around my hand and partway up my arm, trying to protect my skin as best I could. Then, before I could think about it and change my mind, I plunged my covered arm into the garbage can and pulled out a massive handful of debris.

Ashes scattered across the floor and smeared along the hem of my skirt, but I knew I'd found what I'd been looking for. In my hand, I held the singed remnants of a black leather glove.

I laid the glove on the floor and unwrapped my hand

from the towel. Suddenly, my heart was racing. Hadn't I just been wondering about George's ungloved hand the day of the murder? Since that first day, I'd always seen him in brown driving gloves, but he'd been mysteriously barehanded that first day. Had I just solved the mystery of why?

Aside from some singing around the wrist and a hole in the thumb, the glove looked in remarkably good shape for having been set on fire. The material was black, which I was sure hid a good many of the flaws caused by the flames. I wondered why George had sought to destroy it. First, I thought perhaps the glove had been part of a set and he'd dropped one in an incriminating location, but a second peek into the garbage can proved that was not true. The other glove lay at the bottom, in a similar condition to the first. So, I picked up the glove I'd managed to extract with my fingertips, trying to touch it as little as possible, and turned it.

There was a small stain on the back side. It ran across one of the fingers almost like a paint drip. Upon closer inspection, it spread to several of the other fingers, as well. It could have been oil or some other car fluid—I knew remarkably little about cars or car maintenance—but that theory begged the question of why George would have chosen to burn the gloves if they had become ruined by something as commonplace as car fluid?

The towel I'd used to pull the glove from the garbage was already ruined with soot. Since there would be no saving it and returning it quietly back to the shelf from whence it had come, I snatched it up again and dabbed at the stain. Nothing came up. I did it again, pressing harder, smearing across the stain to try and pull anything up. To try and see, at the very least, what color the stain was. My second attempt was more successful. The white fabric of the towel now had a faint smear of rust brown. I knew what dried blood looked like. Immediately, I dropped the towel and the glove to the floor and stepped back.

"Miss Rose?"

I'd been so wrapped up in the glove and the blood, I didn't hear the door open behind me or a man step inside. I only just began to understand the danger I'd put myself in. George had the burned remnants of driving gloves in his room and they were covered in blood. And now, he was in the room with me.

I spun on my heel and pressed myself against the back wall. The still smoldering garbage can was next to me. Residual heat hit my leg like warm, damp breaths.

"What are you doing in here?" he asked.

George didn't look like a murderer. Even then, standing in front of me, his eyes bouncing between my face and the gloves on the floor and the garbage can, he didn't look enraged or violent. He looked scared. I couldn't imagine him harming anyone. Still, I'd learned the hard way that murderers were never who you expected them to be.

"Why were you trying to burn your gloves?" I asked, figuring it would be better to be bold with my line of questioning. There was no point in being shy now. He'd caught me snooping around his room and the evidence he'd sought to destroy was lying at my feet.

He let out a strangled kind of laugh. "I recently received a new pair and I thought I'd get rid of those. I started to burn them, but it was too smoky."

"Why would you burn them?" I repeated.

"I've always had a love of fire," he said, shrugging his shoulders.

That didn't explain away this situation and he knew it. I could tell George was simply hoping I'd drop the matter and leave. I probably should have, but even backed into a corner, I had to ask the questions I'd come there to answer.

"I saw you at the docks the other day," I said, gauging his face for a reaction. "With Frederick Grossmith."

Something flickered behind his eyes at the mention of the dead man's name, but his face remained calm. "I frequent the docks. What day would this have been?"

I slid away from the garbage can, my shoulder-blades dragging along the wall. I wanted to get to the middle of the room and away from the corner so I would have at least two escape routes. George shifted his weight to the left, mimicking my movements.

"The day I arrived in London. The day Frederick Grossmith was murdered," I said.

"I don't know that I've ever met a Frederick—"

"I saw you quarrelling with him." This was not entirely true, but again, I was testing George's reaction.

George's face fell. His thin body sagged forward as though he were carrying around a heavy weight atop his shoulders. "You're right. I don't know how you could know about Frederick, but I was at the docks with him that day."

I gasped. Even though I'd suspected as much, it still felt shocking to hear him admit it out loud.

He took a step towards me, arm extended, and I crushed back against the wall, pulling away from him. Seeing the fear on my face, George folded his arms over his chest, tucking his hands against his sides. "I was with Frederick that morning, but I did not kill him," he said, looking at the floor and shaking his head, as though trying to push away a memory.

"There is blood on your gloves," I said, pointing to the evidence still lying on the floor. "And you tried to burn them. I don't know many innocent men who burn bloody gloves."

"Then you have never met a nervous man," he said, his eyes heavy with sorrow. "Or an innocent one who has much to lose. If there is even a hint of suspicion that I killed Frederick, I could lose this job. The Beckinghams would not keep me around. They have children and a reputation to uphold."

"Are you saying you did not kill the man?" I asked.

He nodded his head quickly, his wavy hair bouncing on top of his head. "Yes, I did not kill him. I fought with him that day, but it was because he came and attacked me. I fought him off and then left. I don't know what happened after that."

I wanted to believe George, but how likely was it that two men could fight and then, minutes later, one of them end up dead by the hand of another party? It seemed like a stretch, to say the least.

"He came and attacked you? Why?"

George sighed. "It's silly, really. Recently, I went out to a jazz club and started up a conversation with the singer. She was an attractive, friendly woman, and I enjoyed her company. What I didn't know was that she was Frederick Grossmith's sweetheart. I'd been to the club a number of times and seen Frederick there. He worked as a bartender, but also liked to cause scenes—fighting and screaming and throwing men out of the club. As soon as I realized I'd stepped on his toes, I apologized and tried to leave, but it was too late. He shouted at me all through the club and into the street, claiming that he would kill me if I ever so much as looked at his girl again. I only stopped in for a quick drink, so I left at the first sign of trouble and planned never to return."

"So, how did you two come to fight at the docks?" I asked.

"He was following me," George said. He placed his hand over his heart. "I arrived a few minutes early to pick you up, Miss, but decided to park a few blocks away from the ship. I didn't want to inhibit the flow of traffic. I was standing next to the car and enjoying the cool air when Frederick blind-sided me. He pressed me against the car and began shouting. People were staring, and I was afraid you or someone who recognized me would see the argument and word would get back to Lord and Lady Ashton. So, I walked down the nearest alley and Frederick followed me, screaming all the while. He had become convinced I was after his girl, though I swore I wasn't. Honestly, Miss, I don't even remember the woman's name."

"When I saw you with him, he shoved you and it looked like things were escalating pretty quickly," I said.

His eyes were wide. "You saw me leave after that, right?"

I shook my head. "No, I'm sorry. The situation seemed dangerous, so I left."

George took another step towards me, his eyes desperate. "He pushed me and I defended myself, Miss. I swear that was the end of it. I punched him and I think it broke his nose. He began bleeding heavily, and I used the opportunity to make my escape. I must have been just moments behind you as you made your escape."

George could be telling the truth, but one fact kept nagging at me. A few minutes after I ran from the alley, Mr. Worthing had sent a police officer to investigate the alley. When the officer arrived at the scene of the argument, he found Frederick Grossmith's body. If George's story was true, it meant that in the three to four minutes between when he left Frederick in the alley with a bloody nose and when the officer arrived, someone else would have had to arrive and shoot Frederick, killing him. The window of opportunity was a small one. I didn't say any of this to George, though. We were still in an uncomfortably small space together, and I didn't want him to know I suspected he might be lying.

"That does not answer the question of why you chose to burn the gloves," I said as gently as possible. "If you were not guilty of the murder, why would you need to destroy them?"

George had been looking at the floor, but he lifted his face just enough so I could see the shadows under his eyes, the lines around his face that, though they had probably been there for many years, looked suddenly deeper. Whether he committed the murder or not, I didn't know, but the incident had not been easy on him. The part of me not consumed with questions and fear pitied him.

"The Beckinghams took a chance on me," he said softly. "I came from a poor family. I have a history of burglaries and other mistakes from my past. My brother went to prison for murder. No one wanted to hire a criminal or the brother of a murderer, but the Beckinghams believed in me. They gave me a job and a home and a life. I burned the gloves because I was afraid of what would happen if anyone even connected me to the scene of the murder. I wanted to put as much distance between myself and the fate of Frederick Grossmith as possible."

He moved as though he were going to lunge forward and I seized up, fear tensing my muscles, but then, at the last second, he collapsed back into an armchair. Dust rose from the upholstery, each speck illuminated in the light from the lamp behind him. Sitting there, George looked like a defeated man.

"I understand if you feel you need to tell someone," he

said, his voice quiet. "But I must also ask you to believe me. I did not kill anyone. I would never. This could cost me my job."

"There is much more on the line than your position with the Beckinghams, if the police find cause to suspect you of the crime," I said.

His already pale face turned a translucent white. I could see the veins running across his forehead and around his eyes. "Are you going to accuse me?"

With George sunken down in his chair, I took the opportunity to move across the room towards the door. I didn't expect he would harm me—if he'd wanted to, he would have already—but I didn't want to take any chances. "I do not yet know you as a person because we have only just met, so I don't know that I can make you any promises on that front," I said. "However, I will take everything you've said into consideration and I will not rush into a decision."

George didn't turn around as I walked to the door, but I could see the back of his head nodding up and down, absorbing what I'd said. "That is as fair a response as I suppose I can ask," he said. "Thank you, Miss Rose."

With that, I backed out of the door, cut across the garden, and dove into the enveloping safety of the main house.

I didn't see anyone as I made my way up to my room, for which I was grateful. Though I'd told George I would not rush into a decision, my face certainly would have given away the thoughts swirling in my mind. Once in my room, I went immediately to the basin in the corner and wetted down my flushed face. The scar on my cheek stood out red and angry against my skin, and once I patted my skin dry, I dabbed on a bit of white powder to dampen the color. Once I felt like myself again—or, as much myself as I would ever be again—I dropped onto my bed, hands over my eyes, and took a few deep, settling breaths.

I'd woken up that morning early, prepared for the day. I would speak to Achilles Prideaux and visit the cemetery. It was more of a cleansing ritual than anything else. I wanted to remove all barriers, physical and emotional, that stood in the way of me achieving what I'd come to London to do. Instead, however, I'd found myself entangled in yet another murder investigation. Because, as much as I didn't want to get involved, I was the only person in the Beckingham household who knew anything about George's connection to the dead man at the docks. If he was a murderer, I was the only person who stood between him and the family I was coming to care about. I would have to either clear his name or prove him guilty.

The police sergeant from two nights before had mentioned that Frederick Grossmith worked at a jazz club, The Chesney Ballroom, which George admitted he had gone to. Perhaps I could go there and talk to the rest of the staff. I could get an idea of whether George's depiction of Mr. Grossmith as a hot-headed, angry man was accurate. And maybe, if I was lucky, someone would have witnessed the initial argument between George Hoskins and Frederick Grossmith. Visiting the club would be the only way to learn about the victim and who might have had a motive to kill him.

I stood up and moved to my closet, shoving everything aside until I found the dress hanging in the back. The dress I'd been certain I would never find occasion to wear. It was all sparkles and fringe, absolutely perfect for a jazz club.

With my dress in order, only one question remained: how would I tell the Beckinghams I'd be missing dinner to go to a jazz club?

11

"You won't be staying for dinner?" Lady Ashton asked, appalled even before mention of the jazz club.

I'd come downstairs in my dress and the entire family had turned to stare at me, open-mouthed. The dress was sleeveless, knee-length, and loose around my waist. Small silver beads were stitched in a radial design, like a silver sun coming from the center of my chest, and the whole ensemble ended with long fringe that flowed to the middle of my calf. I'd matched the dress with a sequined headband and a pair of black t-strap heels. It was far more elaborate than anything I'd ever worn before, and the shock on the faces of my family proved they noticed the difference.

"I'm sorry for the short notice," I said, standing in front of the door to the entrance hall, one foot in the dining room, one foot out.

"Where are you going?" Lord Ashton asked, lowering himself into his seat and sliding into the table. His voice sounded curious, but his face gave nothing away.

I quirked my head to the side as though I had to think about it for a moment. "The Chesney Ballroom, I believe it's called," I said, shrugging my shoulders. I tried to sound casual, but Edward narrowed his eyes at me, making me believe I'd sounded anything but.

"Ballroom?" Lady Ashton asked. "As in, a club?"

"A jazz club?" Alice asked, tucking her legs beneath her so she could more properly lean across the table and take in my outfit. "Are you going to dance?"

"Do they even serve food there?" Lady Ashton asked. Her face was pinched with worry, and it was enough to almost convince me I should stay home. But I'd already done the hard part of telling them where I was going, it would have been silly to back out now.

"Food and drinks," Catherine said, arching an eyebrow at me. I couldn't tell whether it was out of approval or disgust.

"Drinking? A young lady can't go out drinking alone." Lady Ashton turned to her husband, seeking his agreement, and when he didn't respond, I saw her kick him beneath the table.

"Perhaps Edward could go with her," he suggested. "He could ensure the place is respectable and well-suited for a lady."

His wife had clearly been hoping he'd dissuade me from taking the trip at all. Her lips puckered, but she seemed nervous to disregard his idea entirely.

"I'm sure Edward is much too busy to—"

"I wouldn't mind," Edward said. He had already scooted away from the table, and in a surprising turn of events, he was smiling.

I stared at him, waiting for the catch. Waiting for the surprise twist in which he laughed in my face and admitted he actually hoped I would drink so much I'd lose my way home. But it didn't come. He seemed genuinely pleased at the idea.

"Well, I, uh…" Lady Ashton seemed perplexed, and with Lord Ashton, Edward, and myself against her, she was clearly outnumbered. So, she simply closed her lips tightly, turned her attention back to the table, and unfolded a napkin in her lap.

"Have fun!" Alice shouted as we left. "Tell me everything!"

"Alice!" Lady Ashton snapped. "Do not stand up on the furniture."

George drove us to The Chesney Ballroom and Edward seemed content to travel in perfect silence, which suited me just fine. I memorized the turns we took to get there, marking the buildings and houses and distinguishable trees in my mind. George had managed to remain completely stoic while Edward told him where we were headed. I only noticed the tiniest twitch in his hand at the mention of The Chesney Ballroom, and it was only because I'd been looking for it.

When we arrived, big band music and laughter spilled through the open door and onto the street. George stepped around to help me out of the car, but Edward dismissed him, choosing instead to do it himself. He opened my door and extended a hand to me, which I reluctantly took.

"No need to wait for us, George," Edward said. "We'll take a cab home."

"Are you sure, Mr. Edward?" George asked, his eyes flicking to me. "It's no trouble for me to wait."

"Please," Edward said, his voice a bit more clipped. "Enjoy the night off."

As soon as George pulled away, Edward became the

person I'd been expecting from the very start. His smile faded to a sneer and he breezed past me and into the club, never once turning to be sure I was following him. But again, I didn't take issue with any of this. If he preferred to avoid me for the entire evening, then he and I had very similar ideas of what would make for a pleasant evening. I hadn't wanted anyone to accompany me anyway.

I brushed a fingertip across my cheek, hoping the club would be dim enough that my scar wouldn't stand out—not that it mattered much, of course, except for my own vanity —and stepped inside.

It felt like I'd entered another world. Growing up in New York, I'd seen the seedy underbelly of the world. Then, living with the Beckinghams in India, I'd realized how lavish life could be. Servants and personal drivers. Dinner parties and ballgowns. Rose had a different pair of silk pajamas for every day of the week. The Chesney Ballroom, however, seemed to mix both worlds in a dangerous, glittering cocktail.

Dim lights left patches of the room in shadow, and I slipped through them, trying to stay out of everyone's way in the crowded space. Even though I didn't want to speak to him, I found myself looking for Edward. Why had he so readily agreed to join me?

I tried to ignore the blare of the band on stage and the dancers, who were flailing their arms and legs, sending the fringe on their dresses flying up into the air, revealing their stockinged thighs. I focused my thoughts on the task at hand. Edward was here somewhere.

"I found a table."

The hand on my wrist made me jump, and I was prepared to strike out at whoever had grabbed me until I realized it was Edward. The lights in the club made his cheekbones and eye sockets look hollow like a corpse.

My eyebrows pulled together, my brain trying to figure him out even though I'd already decided it was a useless endeavor. I still didn't understand why he had decided to accompany me. Seeing my confusion, he rolled his eyes and pulled harder on my arm.

"You have to eat dinner. If I take you home without food, my mother would never forgive me," he said in a huff.

That was one mystery solved. Edward, despite his tough outer shell, was afraid of his mother's wrath. Perhaps I could use that particular weakness to my advantage.

We sat at a table in the back corner. It offered an excellent view of the entire club, allowing me to take in the patrons and employees without looking too suspicious. A waitress with a dangerously short dress came over and Edward ordered us each baked ham and a gin fizz. The waitress stared longingly at Edward, probably hoping he would flirt with her—something I also would have paid good money to see for myself—before deciding it wasn't going to happen and disappearing through a door in the back wall.

I hadn't noticed the doors at first, but now I could see several of them set into the back of the club. Waitresses moved in and out of one, submitting orders and carrying out plates. Another door in the back corner seemed to be used solely by the dancers, singers, and members of the band. It seemed most likely that was where the dressing rooms and break rooms would be located. If I wanted to speak to the employees without Edward breathing down my neck, that was where I'd have to go.

"Why did you want to come here?"

Edward's voice pulled me from my thoughts, and I

turned to look at him. Only moments before, he had seemed content to pretend I didn't exist, but suddenly he was staring at me. I felt like an animal in a cage, gazing into the eyes of the scientist who hoped to dissect me.

"It seemed like a fun idea," I said, trying to sound casual.

"Fun?" His dark eyebrows shot up.

"Yes, *fun*," I said, placing special emphasis on the word. "My life has been a series of tragedies of late, and I wanted to remind myself what it feels like to be normal."

Edward's mouth twisted to one side. "That sounds like something I would say."

Suddenly, it was my turn to look surprised. "Does it? I can't imagine you being concerned about fun."

"Come on, cousin. Have you forgotten our good times so quickly?" he asked.

My heart leapt in my chest. It was easy to remember my situation when talking with Lord or Lady Ashton or Catherine or Alice. They were all so cordial and polite. Alice had been too little to remember me from her childhood and she only wanted to talk about India. Catherine didn't want to talk at all, which didn't bother me a bit. And Lord and Lady Ashton seemed uncomfortable making any mention of my parents, as if they were afraid I would crumble at the sound of their names. Edward was the only person who seemed set on challenging me, forcing me to prove repeatedly that I was who I claimed to be. If I wasn't careful, he would find me out sooner or later.

"Of course not," I lied. "It is just that you have changed considerably since I last knew you."

I didn't know this for sure, but I did know Rose, and she would not have liked the person Edward was. If they were ever close, it was because Edward was much different back then.

The sly smile he wore faltered a bit, and his posture seemed to go with it. "The stressors of being an adult are more daunting than those of a child. I suppose I am a different person now."

I nodded my head in agreement. "As am I. Responsibilities and life events and time change people."

Edward looked ready to say something, but the waitress reappeared with our dinner and drinks. By the time she left, enough minutes had passed that the conversation felt fractured and stilted. I sipped my gin fizz and cut small slices of ham with my knife and fork, glad for something to keep my nervous hands busy.

"I visited places like this often in school," Edward said, leaning forward to speak over the band. "I was quite the dancer."

"Did all of your many dance partners tell you that?" I teased.

His face darkened momentarily and his eyes narrowed. "I actually only stepped out with one girl while I was in school. Amelie. You remember her, right?"

No, not at all. I never remembered Rose making a single mention of Amelie, but I did my best not to panic. If Edward saw nervousness in my face, he would pounce on it.

I shook my head. "Sorry, I must have forgotten. Being in India made it difficult to stay up to date with the family news."

Edward nodded, though suspicion was painted in thick layers across his face. "I understand, though I'm surprised you don't remember this particular piece of news. You sent me a condolence letter after her funeral."

Funeral? Amelie had died? That was something Rose most certainly would have remembered. Also, it helped explain Edward's constantly sour mood.

"Oh, of course. Amelie," I said, saying the name as though it were the answer to a puzzle I'd been trying to solve. "I'm so sorry. I haven't been quite the same since the accident. My memory comes and goes."

That was a believable excuse, right? It had been an explosion. My cheek had been damaged. There was no way for Edward to know I hadn't suffered some kind of injury to my brain. Plus, even if he suspected I was lying, he wouldn't be able to say it. That was the small benefit of the kind of trauma I'd endured, no one wanted to talk about it.

Edward looked off towards the dance floor and nodded his head a few times, so I knew he'd at least heard me. We had both finished our meals and the waitress hadn't been back to ask whether we wanted more drinks, so my body was humming with unspent energy. I needed to stand up.

"Do you want to dance?" I asked, tipping my head towards the dance floor.

He looked at me, eyes wide, for a second before resuming his neutral expression, standing up, and extending a hand. I took it and he led me to the dance floor.

The rest of the club appeared to be couples, and drunk couples, at that, so the tamped down somberness between me and Edward stood out. Where everyone else was flailing and swirling around the room, we remained contained, moving only as fast as the music required. Even still, it was clear Edward had a fair deal more experience than I did. In direct opposition to his suspicious glances and biting comments, his body moved with grace and confidence around the dance floor. Enough so that he was able to lead me with ease.

After the final spin of an upbeat jazz number, the band quieted and a man stepped up to the microphone.

"Everyone, Everilda Cassel," he said, his voice low and booming.

The crowd cheered and shouted as a petite woman with long, lean muscles moved across the stage to the mic. Her tanned skin paired perfectly with her gold flapper dress. Shimmery beads like bits of pearl and opal were embroidered on the material and caught the stage lights as she moved. Everilda had short curly hair that was slicked back beneath a headband, a few curls strategically coming forward to frame her high cheekbones.

She grabbed the microphone with ease, showing her familiarity with the spotlight, and began to sing. A few notes in, a piano joined her, but she barely needed it. Her voice was smooth and warm. Goosebumps raced up my arms and down my legs as she sang, swaying along with the words. Everyone around us paired off, moving together in the dark to Everilda's voice.

This had to be the woman Frederick had been seeing. George Hoskins told me he'd been speaking with a singer at the club, and so far, she appeared to be the only singer The Chesney Ballroom had.

I'd almost forgotten about Edward, so when he cleared his throat next to me, I jumped.

"Do you want another dance?" he asked.

"Sure," I said, quickly reaching out to grab his hand. I didn't really want to slow dance with my cousin, but I wanted to stay close to Everilda. I wanted to be in the center of the room, so I could easily follow her wherever she went after the song was finished.

"Didn't you used to have a birthmark?"

I looked up at Edward, and it took me a few minutes to comprehend what he was saying. A mark? No, I never had a mark.

But Rose did.

"You showed it to me when we were kids," he continued. "It was on your shoulder. Pretty large, if I remember right. And wine colored."

I nodded, turning slightly to look at my bare shoulder. "Yes, I used to. It faded away years ago, though."

"Did it? I didn't realize birthmarks could fade away with time," he said, his voice trailing off.

Luckily, I was saved a response by a brunette woman in a peach gown. She swirled up next to us and tapped Edward on the shoulder. She couldn't have been more than twenty, but she carried herself with confidence.

"Are you claimed for the next dance?" she asked. Normally I would have found the way she ignored me entirely rude, but she looked smitten with Edward.

"He is absolutely free," I said, disentangling myself from him. "Have fun, cousin."

Edward opened his mouth, but no words came out. I couldn't tell whether he was grateful or annoyed by my act, but I didn't have time to worry about it. Everilda was wrapping up her time on the stage, bowing to the clapping crowd.

As soon as she finished, the full band began to play, filling the club with music that vibrated the floor, and Everilda slipped off the side stage stairs. A few men stopped her as she moved through the club, but she paid them little mind. I trailed her around the edge of the room until she ducked inside the door in the back corner I'd noticed earlier. The one the other performers were coming and going from.

I hesitated outside the door and turned to find Edward. I didn't want him to see me, but it was clear by the way he was staring at his dance partner that he had forgotten about me entirely.

Good, I thought. *Perhaps they'll hit it off and Edward will find a better way to spend his time than trying to catch me in a lie.*

Certain I was in the clear, I reached for the door with confidence, pulled it open, and stepped inside.

12

The hallway I stepped into was dim and filled with smoke. I could hear laughter and voices behind every closed door I passed, but it wasn't until I reached the end of the corridor that I saw Everilda's name on a slip of paper next to a wooden door. I knocked.

"Come in," she shouted, not bothering to answer the door.

I pushed it open to find Everilda sitting in front of a vanity, hair pins sticking out of her mouth as she twisted strands of her hair into place.

"Who are you?" Her voice wasn't angry or accusatory, merely curious.

"Rose," I said, smiling. "You sounded wonderful out there."

"Thank you," she said, clearly flattered. "But customers really aren't supposed to be back here. Tom won't like it."

"Tom?"

She nodded. "Tom Chesney, the owner. It's against the rules, and he's a stickler for rules."

"I'll be quick," I assured her. "I just have a few questions for you."

Suddenly, her body stiffened. Her kind face shifted into a mask. "Is this about Frederick?"

"Oh, well..." I stuttered.

"I already talked to the police," she said, standing up and smoothing out her dress. "I don't have anything else to say."

"I'm not with the police. I have a friend, George Hoskins. He was in here the other night. He said he spoke to you?"

Everilda looked cautious, but the mention of a mutual friend had softened her. "Yeah, I know George. He's been in The Chesney occasionally. We spoke for the first time the last time he was here."

"What did you talk about?" I asked.

It looked like she was prepared to answer my question, but then she stopped, turning her head to the side. "Are you the girl from the alley? The one they say was a witness?"

I wanted to lie, but what good would it do? Clearly, people already knew a woman had witnessed the crime, and then I showed up asking about it. I didn't know much about Everilda, but I didn't assume she'd be dumb enough to see my visit as a coincidence. "Yeah, I am," I admitted.

"I should be the one asking you questions, then," she said. "Didn't you see Frederick get into a fight minutes before being killed? Tell the police who you saw him with and we've as good as solved this case."

"It's not quite that simple," I said, not wanting to go into detail about how complicated the entire situation actually was. Instead, I reclaimed the conversation. I was there to ask the questions. "George said Frederick didn't like him talking to you and caused a scene? He said they got into a fight."

She rolled her eyes. "When didn't Frederick cause a

scene? He was constantly in a fight. It was hard to keep up with."

"He had enemies?" I asked.

She laughed. "I've never met anyone less likeable than Frederick. You'd be hard pressed to find someone he could call a friend."

That seemed harsh. George hadn't said very kind things about Frederick, either, but I'd expected his girlfriend at least to like him. None of this made any sense.

"I'm sorry. Maybe I'm misunderstanding something," I said. "I thought you and Frederick were an item."

Everilda brushed a loose strand of hair behind her ear and shrugged. "We went out a few times.

"Were you two seeing one another at the time of his murder?" I asked, memories surfacing. "Because the argument I overheard had to do with Frederick not wanting George or any other man to speak with you."

She shook her head. "Like I said, we went out a few times over the years that we worked together. Frederick may have believed our relationship to be more than it was, but that isn't any fault of mine."

"I would never seek to blame you," I said.

She continued, talking over me, the words coming out in a heated tumble. "Frederick wasn't as mean to me as he was to everyone else, so I let him hang around me occasionally, but that didn't make me blind. I could see his faults. He had a temper and no way to control it. As sad as it is, I'm not surprised he's dead. It was bound to happen sooner or later."

I nodded, trying to take everything in. Everilda hadn't exactly discounted George as a suspect, but she had given almost every other person in Frederick's life a motive. The man was not nice, and it sounded as though he had given plenty of people reason to want him dead.

"Do you know anyone who may have wanted to kill him? Any recent arguments or fights? Had he mentioned anything to you?" I asked.

"I'll tell you the same thing I told the police when they came around," she said, hand on her hip. "Your friend George wasn't the only person to have a quarrel against Frederick. Our boss didn't much care for him."

"Tom Chesney?" I asked.

"The very same," she said. "Frederick liked to blackmail people. Trust me, I should know. I don't know what he had on Tom, but based on the tension between them, it had to be something good. Otherwise, Tom would have fired Frederick months ago."

"Was he blackmailing you?" I asked. I didn't miss the small aside in the midst of her speech. It sounded as though she knew about Frederick's blackmailing first hand.

"Did you come back here to solve a murder or to try and get me to divulge my secrets?" she asked with a cheeky smile. "I prefer to think my secrets died with Frederick, thank you very much."

I could understand a woman wanting to be the keeper of her own secrets, so I responded with a knowing nod and moved on. "Do you think Frederick was blackmailing anyone else?"

"Honey, we don't have time to go through the whole list," she joked. "But the only other person I can think of is a regular. His name is Artie or something. I'm not sure, but he goes by 'Art.' He and Frederick never liked one another, but a few nights ago, things escalated. Art left here with a black eye and a bloody nose with Frederick shouting at him down the street, telling him to never show his face in here again.

And so far, he hasn't, though he made his own threats that night."

"Art threatened Frederick?"

She nodded. "It was all very cliché. *You'll pay for this. I won't be treated this way.* Nothing that gave me any reason to believe he meant it. Art had been drinking and he and Frederick had fought before. It seemed like just another night at The Chesney."

Everilda spoke of the incident as though it had meant nothing; whereas, I'd seen George and Frederick arguing in the alleyway and run away in terror. Clearly, I wasn't as brave as I liked to think.

"I really need to go," Everilda said, sliding past me and into the hallway. "I have another song in a few minutes, and like I said, Tom won't be happy to find you back here. You should get back into the club."

Everilda began to turn and then stopped, facing me. "Oh, and would you please not mention any of this to anyone?"

"Any of what?" I asked.

"Me and Frederick," she said. "There are already rumors, of course, but I've convinced Tom that is all they were. He has strict rules about employee relationships. I'd be fired if he knew Frederick and I were ever involved."

"Of course. I won't say anything," I promised.

Her lips pulled into a smile that made her squint and then she walked towards the door that led into the club, leaving me alone in her room. I looked around the small space. At the dresses hanging from a pipe on the wall, the shoes piled up on the floor, the thick caking of makeup dust on every surface. She had given me the perfect opportunity to search the room and look for something suspicious, but perhaps that was the exact reason I didn't need to search anything. Everilda clearly had nothing to hide. Plus, I needed to get back before Edward realized I was missing. I'd been gone just long enough that I could reasonably claim I'd been in the ladies room without raising too many eyebrows, but much longer and I'd be pushing it.

As I walked down the hallway, I repeated the names of my suspects, committing them to memory. George. Tom. Art.

George, the chauffeur and Chesney Ballroom regular, who got into a fight with Frederick the night before his murder and again the day of his murder.

Tom, the club owner who was possibly being blackmailed by Frederick.

Art, a regular who'd had run-ins with Frederick in the past and had threatened him shortly before his murder.

Three men with different motives, all with one thing in common: The Chesney Ballroom.

Edward had come with me that night to determine whether the club was respectable, but I was beginning to think it was anything but.

When I got out to the main room, Everilda was walking onto the stage to a round of raucous applause, and Edward was leaning against a wall on the side of the room. He seemed to be enjoying the music. His foot was even tapping along with the beat. As I made my way towards him, he looked up. Immediately, his easygoing expression morphed into a mask of annoyance.

Was it just me? Did I bring out this mean side to him? Or was he this way with everyone? I knew it could have something to do with the fact that I was the only person standing in the way of him inheriting my family's fortune, but that felt extreme. The only way I would have fully understood his anger was if he knew I was lying about being Rose to claim the inheritance for myself. However, if he truly had a suspicion about my identity, certainly he would have said something by now? I had already been to the family solicitor to discuss my monthly payments. The paperwork was signed. It was too late now.

"Where were you?" he asked.

I tried not to let my guilt show. "When I left, you were with a beautiful woman. I didn't think you'd miss my company."

"I'm not here to meet a woman," he snapped. "I accompanied you in order to keep an eye on you, and you disappeared."

"Do not be so dramatic, Edward. I didn't disappear. I'm right here," I said, splaying my arms out and spinning in a small circle.

Edward hummed in the back of his throat. "Are you ready to go?"

"You want to leave?" I asked.

Judging by the expression he gave me next, I assumed his answer was yes. So, to avoid angering him further, I agreed. Before we walked outside, I turned for one last look at Everilda. She had the microphone in one hand, her other arm thrown behind her while she belted out a high note. However, somehow, she managed to look across the room and find me. Our eyes met momentarily, and I turned away quickly, shy under her gaze.

Edward was about to hail one of the cabs lined up on the street when I saw George parked further up the road. I pointed him out.

"That stubborn man," Edward grumbled.

When we got to the car, George jumped out and ran around to open our doors. It looked as though he'd been sleeping, but when his eyes met mine, I could see the question behind them. He wanted to know what I'd discovered. I offered him a smile and little else.

"I told you to go home, George," Edward said, though his voice sounded more amused than disappointed.

"I didn't mind waiting. It's a beautiful night," George said, closing the door behind us.

He moved around to the front of the car and once again he tried to catch my eyes through the window, but I looked down at my lap, playing with the beadwork of my dress. I had a few more leads, but I didn't yet know enough to make George any promises.

13

When Alice had asked me to tell her everything about the jazz club, she'd meant it. It was all she wanted to talk about for days. I tried to impress upon her how ordinary the experience had been, but she wouldn't hear of it.

"I bet it was magical," she said, her eyes dancing with excitement. "Did you meet anyone there?"

"I talked to one of the singers," I said, shrugging my shoulders.

Alice groaned. "No, like a man. Did you meet a man?"

Thankfully, Lady Ashton made an appearance at that moment and I was spared answering Alice's invasive question, at least for the time being.

Edward barely acknowledged my presence in the days after we returned from the jazz club. He stopped watching me from his bedroom window and interrogating me over meals. He wasn't exactly nice or polite, but it was still a vast improvement. And George seemed to be more at ease around me. Every day that passed without his being arrested or fired, he relaxed a bit. I still hadn't decided what I planned to do about what I knew, but it was nice to not feel him staring at me every time we took the car anywhere.

All of that, though, took a backseat to my main focus: Achilles Prideaux. I'd called his number two days after my night at The Chesney Ballroom and he had finally picked up.

"Mademoiselle Rose?" he'd asked, doubt filling his voice.

"Yes, from the ship," I said. "Rose Beckingham."

"I did not expect you to call," he said.

"I did not expect to call," I responded truthfully.

He agreed to meet me the next morning over breakfast. After a restless night of sleep, I rose early the next day, dressed in a sage green tea dress with loose sleeves that hung down to my elbows and a cream cloche hat that matched my heels, and set out early. I didn't want anyone in the family, George included, to know where I was going, so I walked a few blocks to the main road and hailed a cab.

This time, when I knocked on Monsieur Prideaux's door, he answered after the first knock.

"Mademoiselle Beckingham," he said, arms spread wide, as if he were going to hug me, though he stayed firmly on his side of the threshold.

He looked tanner than he had the last time I'd seen him, though he still sported the same thin, black mustache. And I still detested it.

"Monsieur Prideaux," I responded, smiling. "It is good to see you again."

"Please, come in." He stepped aside, and I walked into his house.

It looked nothing like I'd expected—partly because I'd

expected him to live in a one-bedroom flat with blacked out windows and a single spotlight shining down on a metal chair where he interrogated people. Of course, he actually lived in a spacious two-bedroom flat with an abundance of household plants scattered amongst his full bookshelves and artwork. Morning light poured through his open windows, giving the place a light, airy feel.

"You have a beautiful home."

He laughed. "You sound surprised."

"Wow, you are a word-class detective," I teased. "When did you get back from Aden?"

"Yesterday morning. I'd only been home a few hours when you called."

"I hope I am not inconveniencing you by calling so soon after your arrival home," I said.

"Of course not. If you were, I would have told you so," he said, smiling. "Though I suspect the feeling may be one-sided, I quite enjoy your company, Mademoiselle."

Achilles directed me to take a seat at his dining room table. He poured two cups of tea and then took the seat across from me. "I assume you are not here to discuss home décor."

"Correct," I said. "I'm actually in need of your help."

I paused, but he quickly gestured for me to continue. All business.

"I need you to find a missing person for me. A person from my past."

"In Bombay or London?" he asked. All of his easygoing charm and playfulness had disappeared. I was now speaking to the famous detective Achilles Prideaux, not my casual acquaintance.

"Neither, actually," I said, my fingers pulling nervously at the material of my dress. "New York."

I could tell this piqued Monsieur Prideaux's interest, but he simply nodded and let me continue.

"His name is Jimmy. The last time I saw him, which was over ten years ago, he had blonde hair that curled around his ears, freckles across the bridge of his nose, and a lean frame, though I'm sure he is much taller now."

"Not unlike yourself, then?" Monsieur Prideaux asked.

I nodded and bit my lip. "Yes, not entirely unlike me."

"Where did you last see Jimmy?"

"Five Points, New York City," I said, doing my best not to linger on the fact.

At this, Achilles did little to hide his surprise. "That is a rough area. I wasn't aware you had ever travelled in the United States."

The fact was that I did not have to answer any of his questions if I did not want to. This was not a police investigation. I was questioning him, which meant I could choose to skip over any information I chose. Therefore, I chose not to answer this particular inquiry and moved on.

"After I saw him last, I found a locket Jimmy had once given me. Nearby, he'd left a single scrap of torn paper with two words scribbled on it: help me. After that, he disappeared. It has been many years since I received that note. I was only a child then, but now I am grown and I have the means to find him, so I would like to try."

"Do you have the note?"

My heart ached at the loss. "No, unfortunately I do not. I recently lost the locket."

Achilles twisted his mouth to one side, his thin mustache turning into a scribble on the right side of his face. "I need more information."

I shook my head. "I'm afraid I cannot tell you much more."

"Then I'm afraid I cannot help you," he said flatly.

The words surprised me, and I leaned back in my seat, practically blown over by his words. "You cannot help me?"

"You are hiding something from me," Monsieur Prideaux said. "I've known from the moment I met you that there is more to you than meets the eye, but back on the ship I did not wish to pry. Now, though, if I am to help you, you have to tell me everything."

"What would you like to know?" I asked, growing angry. "I will tell you all I can."

"What was a wealthy English heiress doing in an impoverished New York neighborhood as a child? What is your relationship to the Jimmy you seek?"

Those were two questions I could not answer without telling him my entire history. I would have to reveal my true name and identity. I would have to confess that I had stolen Rose's inheritance away from the family I was now living with in order to use it to carry out this search. Two facts which, if discovered, could see me abandoned and penniless on the street. However, if I did not tell him, then Monsieur Prideaux would not help me and everything I'd endured would be for nothing.

I felt trapped in a cycle of lies and deceit that I could no longer find my way out of. Silence was my only option.

Achilles Prideaux noted my tight lips and shoved away from the table, standing tall and buttoning his suit jacket. "I'm afraid that is all I can do for you, then, Mademoiselle Beckingham."

"Are you too noble to accept my money?" I asked, anger and frustration overflowing.

"It is not my habit to accept clients who conceal the truth from me," he said. "I know this Jimmy is important to you, whoever he may be, but I cannot become involved in something I do not understand. As a private detective, I already have a precarious relationship with the police. If I take on a case that has criminal roots, I will find myself in more trouble than I wish. I am sorry, Mademoiselle, I really am. But I will not be able to help you until you are willing to tell me more."

"I assure you my inquiry is wholly innocent. I simply need to learn the whereabouts of the man I described," I said.

"Do you believe most criminals admit to being criminal?" he asked, a sad smile playing on his lips. "This business has taught me to take no one at their word."

"Not even a friend?" I asked.

"Not even friends," he said, and then after a long pause, continued. "Or acquaintances."

I knew we weren't really friends, but he was the closest thing I had in the city, and it stung to be told so clearly where our relationship stood.

"Then we have nothing further to discuss," I said, pushing away my tea so violently some of it spilled onto the cream tablecloth. I immediately wanted to apologize, but stubbornness held my tongue. Achilles looked at the stain but didn't say anything.

"Let me show you out." He led me back through his small, yet orderly home, and I stepped back out onto the landing where, only a few minutes before, I had been so hopeful.

I wanted to storm off in anger, but hopelessness had begun to creep in. I turned back to him, studying his narrow face, his thin mustache. "Will you really not help me?" I asked.

His gaze was apologetic and yet resolute. "You know where to find me, Mademoiselle Beckingham. Call upon me anytime."

With that, he closed the door between us, and I stepped back out onto the street.

14

I walked the streets for most of the morning. I knew the Beckinghams would worry about me. Lady Ashton was probably beside herself with concern. I hadn't even left a note as to my whereabouts. However, I couldn't bring myself to go home. Not just yet. It would be impossible to go back and sit through lunch and tea and hold polite conversation with the anger and frustration that was coursing through me.

Why wouldn't Achilles Prideaux help me? He'd explained his side of things. Of course, he couldn't become involved in a criminal affair, but why wasn't my promise that I was involved in no such thing enough to reassure him? What had I ever done to make him doubt me?

Anger led to frustration, which led to despair. How would I find Jimmy now? My plan had hinged on gaining Monsieur Prideaux's help. And he was supposed to be a world-famous detective. I could always hire another detective, but with the money the search would cost, I wanted to be certain I was paying for the best. And unfortunately,

Achilles Prideaux was the best. Everyone else would be a poor imitation.

I found myself in front of The Chesney Ballroom before I could even ascertain where my feet were taking me. I didn't know my way around London yet, so my feet had simply walked the streets they recognized. It was barely lunch time, but a sign next to the jazz club's door listed it as open, and I had nowhere else to go. My feet hurt from walking and I had skipped breakfast to talk with Monsieur Prideaux. I was famished for lunch. I had enough money in my clutch for a small something, and a small something was significantly better than nothing, so I pushed through the door and stepped into the dim room.

The place was practically empty, save for a bored bartender wiping down the wooden bar and a man sweeping the floors. I was the only patron, and I was about to turn around and leave when a voice called out to me.

"Sit wherever you like," the man said. He stepped forward until he was standing directly beneath one of the overhead lights, which cast long shadows over his eye sockets and across his mouth, giving him an almost ghoulish appearance. He had a mess of white hair on top of his head, adding to the effect.

I smiled at him, wringing my hands in front of me. I had never been to a restaurant by myself before. Prior to living with Rose and the Beckinghams in India, I hadn't had the money for such a thing. And once I was in India, I accompanied the Beckinghams to functions occasionally, but I never had the time or opportunity to go out on my own. I felt oddly vulnerable. I could choose the table next to the bar, but that put me much too close to the bartender, who might decide to strike up a conversation. There was a small table in the back corner, but it seemed antisocial to sit as far away from every human in the room as possible. And the tables in the center of the room were under the harshest light, and I felt as though I would feel like an exhibit at the museum.

"Or I can choose for you," the man said, clearly annoyed with my indecision.

I felt my face flush as I moved to a table near the bar, deciding it would be better to err on the side of awkwardness than sitting too far away and seeming rude.

The man handed me a menu and then lingered next to my table, arms crossed over his chest.

I glanced up at him several times, wishing he would walk away and leave me to make my decision.

"We don't normally have people in here so early," he said rather grumpily.

I didn't respond for a few seconds and then looked up to see him staring directly at me.

"Oh," I said in surprise. I hadn't expected to be engaged in conversation. "I was just walking by and noticed you were open."

He couldn't very well be angry I had come in when the sign declared they were open. If he didn't want patrons, then he shouldn't have turned the sign. I kept all of that to myself, however.

The man grunted in response.

Even with his pressuring gaze, I managed to select a simple sandwich off the menu, and when he asked what I wanted to drink, I opted for a water.

"Can we at least put a lemon in that for you?" he asked. "It will give Joseph something to do." He pointed over his shoulder at the bartender who was stacking up glasses in a pyramid shape.

"Sure," I said, smiling, hoping I could melt the man's heart with kindness.

"Water with a lemon," he said, snapping.

The bartender jumped into action. "Sure thing, Tom."

Tom? As in, Tom Chesney?

I was surprised to hear the grouchy older man who had grumbled at me the entire time he took my order was the owner of the restaurant. Based on his personality, however, I was not surprised to learn he was one of the suspects in Frederick Grossmith's murder. He hadn't struck me as a particularly kind person. Or a particularly patient one.

I needed to talk to him. I couldn't pass up this opportunity. I was one of the only people in the entire club and the owner was milling around the room by himself. I felt certain I wouldn't get another chance like this one to talk with him. The bartender, Joseph, brought me my water with lemon, and I smiled at him, trying to figure out how I would broach the subject of Frederick's murder in a way that wouldn't make Tom suspicious.

I hadn't yet come up with an idea when Tom pushed through the swinging doors that led into the kitchen and headed towards my table with my plate. He dropped it onto the table in front of me and stood back.

"Anything else I can do for you?" he asked. I was surprised his words could be so polite, yet the question could still sound so insincere.

"This all looks delicious," I said, smiling up at him.

He nodded and turned away, and I panicked.

"Tom?"

He turned at the sound of my voice, his eyebrows pulled low over his eyes, suspicious. "Who's asking?"

I laughed nervously. "Sorry, my name is Rose Beckingham."

His mouth was a stern, straight line. "Who are you to me?"

"We do not know one another, if that is what you're asking."

"Yet, you seem to know me," he said.

"Well, the club is named after you, isn't it?" I asked.

He nodded but said nothing else.

"I recently heard some sad news that involved your club," I said. "That is when I learned your name."

"What news would that be?" he asked.

I would have thought the death of an employee would be big news, but apparently Tom didn't think so.

"An employee of yours was recently murdered, correct?" I asked. "Or, at least, that's what I heard."

"Where did you hear that?" he asked, crossing his arms over his broad chest.

"The police questioned me as a witness in the murder, and I believe the officer mentioned the victim's place of employment."

At this, he raised his eyebrows. "You witnessed the murder?"

"No, not exactly," I said. "I was near the scene of the crime. I saw Frederick arguing with another person, but I left before he was killed."

Tom nodded and then shook his head. "Good thing you didn't stick around. There may have been two murders," he said.

"Do you think so?" I asked. Somehow, I had never considered that possibility. That I could have been one of the victims if I hadn't left when I did. The idea sent a chill down my spine.

He shrugged his large shoulders. "There is no way to know for sure, but you should consider yourself blessed. No one wants to be witness to a grisly crime like that."

"Do you know that from experience?" I asked, rather indelicately.

Tom raised an eyebrow at me. "No, but I can imagine. Can't you?"

"I suppose I can," I said, briefly recalling the image of Rose's severed hand sitting in the seat next to me after the explosion, blood dripping down the leather interior.

"I would have liked to see who pulled the trigger, though," I said. "It would have been nice to give Frederick justice."

"A lot of people think Frederick got his justice," Tom said flatly.

"You mean people think he deserved to die?" I asked, surprised Tom would admit such a thing.

"Some people," he nodded.

"Are you one of those people?"

Tom jutted his lip out defiantly. "Let's just say I didn't consider Frederick to be an upstanding citizen. When you live the way he did, you take your life in your own hands."

I was suddenly grateful I never knew Frederick. I'd talked to three people who did know him and none of them seemed particularly sad about his death. He seemed like trouble.

"Why did you hire him if you felt that way?" I asked.

"Well, I didn't know he was no good when I hired him," Tom said. "He proved himself to be trouble over time."

"How so, if you don't mind my asking?" My sandwich sat in front of me, all but forgotten. I'd come into the club to rest and find something to eat, but now food was the furthest thing from my mind.

Tom pulled out the chair opposite me and lowered himself into it with a sigh. "I suppose it doesn't much matter if I tell you, now that he is dead. Frederick was stealing from me."

I gasped, surprised that he would reveal such information to me, a stranger. "How do you know?"

"Well," he said, shifting in his seat. "I don't know for certain, but I've had my suspicions for a while. It was never a lot of money missing, just small amounts here and there. But it happened often enough that I began to take notice every night Frederick worked the bar. I never caught him in the act. Now that he is dead, I haven't had any money go missing. So, that as much as confirms his guilt in my mind. Though, of course, it doesn't matter now. No justice in it for me."

"Why didn't you confront him?" I asked, riveted. If Tom really believed Frederick was stealing money from him, that could have been his motive. Perhaps, Tom had accused Frederick and things had gone poorly. Bad enough that he killed him.

Tom folded his hands on the table in front of him and leaned forward, leveling his gaze at me. "When I hire someone, I give them my trust. I promise to treat them fairly. Accusing them of thievery or anything else without proof wouldn't be fair. I wanted to be certain before I even considered confronting him." He leaned back. "Even though I didn't have solid proof, I did feel rather confident Frederick was behind the missing money, so I planned to fire him when he showed up for work. But then he never showed up, and the police arrived instead, bringing news that he had died."

"Do you know if Frederick had any enemies?" I asked.

Much like Everilda had, Tom laughed. "The man was not very popular. It would take much less time to list all of his friends."

"Anyone who stood out recently?" I reached for my sandwich and took a bite, trying to make the conversation seem as casual as possible.

"Are you with the police or something?" Tom asked.

Clearly, nonchalance was not my strong suit. "No. I just feel connected to the case because of my proximity to the time and place of the crime." *And the fact that my family's chauffeur may be the murderer.*

Tom nodded, not looking wholly convinced, but comfortable enough to answer my questions. "No one especially stands out, but I do know Frederick and Arthur Burton had another run-in recently."

"Arthur Burton?" I repeated.

"Yeah. I suppose most people know him as Artie. He and Frederick were always at one another's throats over one thing or another. Artie liked to drink and occasionally he would get carried away with some of the female customers, pawing at them when he shouldn't be, and then skipping out on his bill at the end of the night."

"He wouldn't pay? Why would you let him back in if he didn't pay?" I asked.

"He always settled up before we let him back in," Tom said. "Frederick would hunt him down and get the money. Even if he was a thief, that's one thing I'll miss about Frederick. He was never afraid to track people down and get any money the club was owed."

I wondered whether Frederick's penchant for tracking down debtors wasn't what got him killed. If he had sought out Artie for payment, who knew what could have happened?

"He went to Artie's house to force him to pay?"

"Went to his girl's house, more likely. Artie's usually hanging around the place at the end of the next block. Old brick house with a faded blue door," Tom said, standing up. "It's been nice to talk with you, but I have a few things left to do before our afternoon customers come in. Is there anything else I can get for you?"

Tom's question seemed much more genuine this time around, and I wondered whether his tone had really changed or whether my perception of him had.

"No, I have absolutely everything I need," I said, smiling up at him. "Thank you."

He bowed his head once and disappeared into the kitchen.

Once he was gone, I realized how hungry I was. I tucked into my sandwich, finishing the whole thing in less than ten bites, making me glad there was no one else in the club to witness my unladylike manners. Then, I left a few bills on the table and a tip in the bartender's jar on my way out.

Just as I reached the door, a familiar figure came walking out of the door to my right—the door that led to the employee and performer break rooms.

I lifted a hand in greeting to Everilda, but the moment she saw me, the easy confidence in her face turned to stone. Her ruby red lips tightened and she pivoted and disappeared back down the hallway. I stood in the doorway, stunned. What had changed since the last time I'd spoken to her?

I turned around and saw Tom standing at the bar. Perhaps, she was afraid of what Tom would think if he saw her getting friendly with the girl who had asked all the questions? I didn't know the answer, and standing dumbstruck in the doorway to the club wouldn't provide any solution, so I stepped out onto the sidewalk and turned right.

I couldn't entirely explain what was compelling me to try and solve Frederick's murder anymore. Part of it was the fact that the family's chauffeur could have been the murderer, but deep down, I didn't truly suspect him of the crime. If he had done it, wouldn't he have tried to dispose of me when he found me trespassing in his room and I discovered the bloody gloves? I had all the evidence I needed to at least accuse him of the crime, if not entirely convict him of it. That would have been enough reason for him to kill me right then and there. However, he hadn't. So, what made me want to keep going?

If I was being honest with myself, part of it was a distraction. A distraction from the seemingly endless series of obstacles I'd faced. The first of which was losing my locket. The cheap jewelry didn't exactly hinder my plan at all, but it had been a constant in my life for as long as I could remember, and I felt a little lost without it. The second had been receiving my inheritance in installments rather than all at once. While still in India, I'd doubted my plan. Mostly, I'd doubted my ability to maintain the charade of being Rose full time while living with her family members. To keep calm, I'd reminded myself that I could always claim the inheritance and then move away. No one would blame Rose for choosing a solitary life after surviving the trauma she'd suffered. I could take the money and start over someplace where no one knew the name Beckingham. I could go back to being Nellie Dennet if I wanted. Or someone else. I could be whoever I wanted. But now, without the full sum at my disposal, I had to stay in London. I had to stay in contact with the family's solicitor. I no longer had the option of disappearing. And finally, the biggest blow of all, I lost the help of Achilles Prideaux. Now, I had no idea how to go about finding Jimmy's whereabouts.

Whatever the true reason, though, I found myself headed towards the brick house with the faded blue door

Tom had described. It stood one block to the East of The Chesney Ballroom, on the corner. As I walked up, I noticed a blonde man standing on the front steps, banging on the door. I slowed my walk to a crawl.

"Let me in," the man shouted, pounding his fist against the ancient door.

I heard a woman's muffled voice respond, but I couldn't make out any of the words.

"Baby, it was nothing," the man said, sounding considerably softer this time. He leaned against the flaking wood, his cheek squished.

I felt uncomfortable listening to what was clearly an intimate moment, but I couldn't walk away. I needed to know who I was looking at. Was this man Arthur Burton?

Slowly, the door cracked open and a woman with long brown hair pulled into a twist at the base of her neck popped her head out. Her large eyes were focused and sharp, unforgiving.

"You promised me, Arthur," she reprimanded. "You swore to me, and I believed you. I'm not sure which of us is the bigger fool, but either way, I'm tired of being lied to. I'm tired of being fooled by you."

Arthur reached out to stroke the woman's cheek, but she pulled her face away, diving back into the darkness of the house, the door still open.

"It was only one drink, sweetheart," he said, shrugging and looking down at his shoes. "There was more water than vodka in it, I swear."

"You *swore* you wouldn't have any vodka at all," she snapped. "But you can't stay away from that stupid club. Spending time with me is always second to drinking and partying. And Artie? I'm tired of coming second."

Artie shook his head the entire time she spoke. "You aren't second. You are first, Lissa. My number one."

"Then how come I sat on my sofa in my favorite red dress waiting for you to come pick me up all last night and you never showed?" she asked.

Artie opened his mouth to answer, but Lissa kept talking. Apparently, she didn't really want Artie to answer her questions.

"And where were you two days ago when you promised to come over and help me paint the sun porch? And," she added, her voice growing louder through the crack in the door, though I still couldn't see her, "where were you at the beginning of the week when you promised to go with me to pick up my mother from the ship? We had to carry her luggage by ourselves and I ripped my good stockings."

This caught my attention. The ship? Could she mean the *RMS Star of India*? The same ship I'd come in on the day Frederick Grossmith was murdered? Arthur was supposed to meet his fiancé that morning but hadn't shown up. So, where had he been instead?

"I told you," Arthur said, his words coming from behind clenched teeth. "I got caught up."

Lissa cut him off. "I'm tired of your excuses, Artie. And we're causing a scene."

I couldn't see her any more, but she must have gestured towards the street because Artie turned to look in my direction. I quickly picked up my walking pace and stared at the ground, trying to make it look as though I hadn't been eavesdropping on their entire conversation.

Artie turned back around. "I don't care about what anyone else thinks," he said. "I just want to make it up to you."

"You're not welcome here anymore, Art. Goodbye." With

that, Lissa slammed the door shut, leaving Artie once again standing on the front steps, banging against the wood.

I moved down the street quickly, forcing myself not to turn back and study Arthur, which proved to be incredibly difficult. Had I just passed by his house—or Lissa's house—at the exact moment Lissa was explaining that Arthur had no alibi for the time of Frederick's murder? Could I truly be that lucky?

The facts were: Arthur frequented The Chesney Ballroom and had argued with Frederick recently; he had ample opportunity to have committed the murder and escaped quickly; and he was supposed to meet Lissa the morning of the murder, but never showed.

I needed to talk to Arthur somehow. Or Lissa. Because I was pretty sure I'd just found my new main suspect.

15

W hen I finally made it home, Lady Ashton was in hysterics.

"I was moments away from alerting the police, Rose," she chastised, alternating between pulling me in for a hug and shaking my shoulders.

"I'm sorry, aunt. I never intended to scare you," I said.

"Where have you been?" she asked. "I woke up and you weren't in your room. I had the entire house searched for you, yet you were nowhere to be found. You didn't leave a note or tell anyone where you had gone."

"I went for an early morning walk and then stopped for a bite to eat," I said, offering up a half-true, yet flimsy explanation.

"A walk that lasted halfway into the afternoon?" she asked, dubious.

I nodded. "I visited the cemetery," I said.

This was a direct lie, but I knew no one would fault me for spending so much time alone if that time had been spent in mourning. I didn't think she or anyone else could blame me for going to see the headstone that had been erected in honor of my parents.

This theory proved correct when Lady Ashton's face morphed into a mask of pity, her eyes drooping down forlornly. "Oh dear," she said, wrapping me up in another long hug.

"I'm all right," I assured her, patting her on the back. "It was nice to see the headstone. Thank you for having it commissioned."

She smiled at me, her eyes glassy with unshed tears. "Of course, dear. We miss your parents terribly."

Once my fake trip to the cemetery was offered up as an excuse for my absence, no one else mentioned it to me, and I was free to go about my day unhindered. I begged out of afternoon tea with the explanation that I was weary from my walk and would love to lie down, so I spent the better part of the afternoon in my bedroom. I did actually manage to take a short nap, but most of the day was spent in thought about how I would ever locate Jimmy without Achilles Prideaux's help and how I could casually speak with Arthur Burton or his ex-fiancé, Lissa, about Arthur's connection to Frederick and his whereabouts the morning of Frederick's murder.

After Monsieur Prideaux had saved my life aboard the *RMS Star of India*, I had felt us to be something akin to friends. Although I still knew little about his life and he knew even less about mine, the experience felt as though it had bound us together somehow. Rose had been one of my only friends, and I had lost her in the accident. So, it had been nice to think that I had found at least someone who was practically a friend in Achilles Prideaux. However, Achilles had quickly relieved me of that childish notion. He had referred to us as little more than acquaintances, words which, while they had wounded me rather more deeply than I cared to admit, also helped pull me from the pit of despair I'd allowed myself to fall into that morning. The truth was that Achilles and I *were* acquaintances. I had only known him a few short weeks, whereas my plan to locate Jimmy had been in motion before I even met the Frenchman. I had planned to come to London, retrieve Rose's inheritance, and use the money to find Jimmy before I had ever heard a whisper of the famed Detective Prideaux. So, I now realized his refusal to help me should not hinder my search.

A couple hours before dinner, I was feeling much more positive than I had been that morning. I'd finally climbed out of bed, prepared myself for dinner, and with help from the restorative nap I'd taken, was ready for a few laps around the back garden. I was on my way down the back stairs when I heard footsteps behind me and turned to see Catherine running after me.

I had spent little time with Catherine since arriving in London. The few words she'd spoken to me had been harsh and unforgiving, and she seemed intent upon disliking me, so I did little to convince her otherwise. Now, however, it was clear she wanted to speak to me.

She wore a long silk gown that emphasized the delicacy of her tall frame, and her hair was curled into perfect waves that hugged her oval face and made her already large eyes look even more prominent.

"We missed you at afternoon tea, cousin," Catherine said, offering me what appeared to be a genuine smile.

"Ah, yes. I was tired after my adventure this morning."

"You had the house in a bit of a stir," she said with a laugh. "Though, no one was as concerned as Mama. She can work herself into a right tizzy over nothing."

"Sorry if I caused you any trouble," I said.

Catherine reached out a hand and placed it on my shoulder, pursing her lips. "Do not apologize, Rose. My mother told me you visited your parents at the cemetery, and I can only imagine what an emotional experience that must have been for you."

I suddenly felt guilty that this tender moment between Catherine and I was entirely based on a lie. Of course, I *had* visited Rose's parents at the cemetery, just not that morning. And it *had* been an emotional experience, but not for the reason Catherine believed. While living in India, I was close to Rose's family, but her parents never treated me as family the way Rose did. Rose had become like a sister to me, whereas her parents were always more like my employers than anything else. The emotions I felt while visiting their memorial site were linked to the guilt I felt at taking Rose's identity. At the thought that Rose would not receive the proper memorial she deserved.

I swallowed down my guilt and smiled at Catherine. "Thank you, cousin. It was emotional, but the cemetery was quite beautiful. A fitting location for their memorial."

Catherine smiled at me again, though this time, it appeared as though she wished to say more. She bit her lip and looked down at the floor, her hand still resting on my shoulder. I didn't want to turn and walk away but standing with her in silence was too uncomfortable to bear.

"Well," I said, turning slightly.

"Wait."

Catherine dropped her hand and crossed her arms over her chest. She took a deep breath, and suddenly I was more nervous than ever. Catherine always appeared to be wholly confident. She moved through life with an ease and grace brought on by wealth and status. If she was nervous to say something to me, then I didn't even want to imagine what could be the cause. I swallowed down fear while I waited for her to gather the courage to speak.

"Yes?" I prompted, looking up at her.

She pursed her lips together and then began to speak quickly, the words rushing out all at once. "I feel I must apologize for my behavior towards you since your arrival. I have been unkind, and I see now it was unwarranted. I hope you can forgive me."

Whatever I'd imagined Catherine would say, it hadn't been anything close to an apology. I stared up at her, dumbstruck.

She must have taken my silence as anger, for she continued.

"You must understand, we haven't been in one another's confidence in many years, so your sudden arrival was rather unexpected. And, of course, you know that. Leaving India was unexpected, and I know you have been through a trauma, but the root of my anger stemmed from our disintegrated relationship. You and I were good friends when you lived in London, were we not? I considered us as close as sisters. When you left, I expected to remain so."

"Oh," I finally managed to say, the rest of my words caught in my chest. Catherine was angry because Rose had stopped being her friend? I'd taken her anger to be because she missed out on my inheritance or because I was stealing attention away from her. Never had I imagined she could be complex enough to desire my friendship.

"I simply wished to apologize for my behavior and beg your forgiveness. I plan for things to be much different moving forward," she said, nodding her head in earnest.

"Oh," I said, still stunned. "Yes, all right."

"So, you forgive me?" she asked, eyebrows pulled together in doubt.

I reached out to still her nervous hands, which were pulling at the silk of her dress. "Yes, dear cousin. Of course, I do."

The smile that lit up her face could have been a substitute for the sun. She was beaming, and I felt a sudden kinship with her that I hadn't felt in the entire time I'd been in London. Then, suddenly, her face fell again. Worry darkened her eyes.

"I feel I must apologize for something else, as well," she said, barely daring to look up at me.

I squeezed her fingers, reassuring her. "Yes?"

She sighed. "Well, Edward was dubious when word of your miraculous survival reached us, and I fear I encouraged his disbelief. We had thought you dead for several days, and then suddenly you were alive, and everyone was thrilled and talking at length about having you at the house. Jealousy sparked inside me, and though I see how silly my feelings were now, they did not feel silly at the time. I allowed myself to be controlled by envy, and it has now created a large chasm between you and my brother."

My heart felt as though it were lodged in my throat. Had I not been holding on to Catherine's hand, I might have tumbled backwards down the stairs. "So, Edward does not believe I truly survived?" I asked, my lips dry as a desert. "I'm afraid I do not understand."

"In short, he believes you are not our cousin, Rose Beckingham," Catherine said, shaking her head. "Please do not be angry with him. I know how it must feel, but he has been going through a hard time. Not as difficult as yours, of course, but then very few people experience the kind of misfortune you have, dear cousin. Edward is the eldest child and the only son of my parents. He went to school but has done nothing with his education and has few prospects. Our family, if I may be honest with you, is approaching uncertain financial circumstances in the future. Nothing that will ruin us, mind you. Perhaps Edward and I have exaggerated that a bit. But things are tighter than they used to be. Although news of your family's tragedy shook us to our core, there was also talk of the inheritance, and I'm afraid Edward may have taken to the idea of having the money. As sad as the circumstances were, the money would have helped us. When word of your survival reached us, Edward didn't want to believe it right away."

Somehow, it was a comfort to me that Edward had begun to doubt my identity even before seeing me. It meant my disguise was better than I thought. His disbelief didn't stem from my appearance or memories—though, that certainly could have been fueling his fire—but from his own greed.

"I'm not angry," I said. Quite the contrary, in fact. I felt a renewed sense of peace. I had begun to believe that perhaps Edward and Catherine doubted my true identity, but to hear Catherine say she believed me to be Rose all along and that she had, in actuality, encouraged Edward's disbelief gave me hope that he could be persuaded. That he could come to believe I was his cousin. "Thank you for your apology, but I assure you it is unnecessary. I'm only sorry we lost touch over the years."

Catherine smiled down at me. "You are as kind as ever, dear Rose."

16

I had half an hour until dinner, so I decided to spend it out of doors. The day had turned a comfortable kind of warm and the dappled afternoon sunshine coming through the trees eased away my worries. Walking amongst the flowers and the foliage of the garden, I felt like I could finally breathe.

Edward, who usually would have been watching me from the window in his bedroom, had been out of the house all day. I noted with some annoyance that he had also left early that morning without telling anyone where he planned to be, yet Lady Ashton only worried about me. I thought often that my mission would be much easier to accomplish if I was a man. No one seemed to concern themselves with the comings and goings of men, but women were to be watched and monitored at all times for their own safety. Regardless, Edward's absence allowed me to wander from the back of the house to the front freely, enjoying the sight of people walking home after a long day, and appreciating the solitude of the back garden simultaneously.

I was rounding the side of the house for the third time

that evening when I saw a man approaching from the street. His head was down, so I could only see the top of his cap and his dark gray suit. However, when he did finally lift his head, the breath left my body in one disbelieving sigh.

Arthur Burton was moving up the walkway towards Ashton House, carrying a small package under his arm.

My mind flitted between two questions: What was he doing here? What did I plan to do about it?

Getting the answer to the first was wholly dependent on my answer to the second. I could do the brave thing and march up to him, ask what he was doing at my home, and then question him about the death of Frederick Grossmith. Or I could do what I desperately wanted to do: escape into the back garden and dive into the relative safety of the house.

I was standing at the corner of the house, half-exposed to anyone who would be at the front, when my decision was made for me. Arthur looked in my direction, spotted me, and raised a hand in greeting. So as not to look like a peeper who resided in the bushes, I raised my hand in return and moved towards him.

"Can I help you?" I asked, hoping the tremor in my voice wasn't obvious.

"I'm looking for a," he glanced down at the package in his arms, "Rose Beckingham."

"I am she," I said.

Did he know I suspected him of the crime? Was he here to deliver a package laced with poison? Or worse, when I reached for the package, would he strike out and cut my throat? Horrible possibilities flashed through my mind in the few seconds it took for Arthur to extend the package toward me with one hand. Despite the panic bubbling up inside of me, threatening to take hold of my mind and body, I calmly reached out and took it from him.

I breathed. Once. Twice. Three times.

Nothing happened. The package didn't explode into flames or make my eyes burn or my skin flake off. It seemed like a completely innocuous item, which surprised me more than if the parcel had been dangerous. What was Arthur doing here if not to dispose of me for being a witness to the crime I was growing increasingly more confident he had perpetrated?

"I found a necklace near The Chesney Ballroom, the jazz club. And when I went to turn it in to the police, someone told me where I could find you," he said.

I nodded, trying to understand. He'd found a necklace and someone had sent him to me? Then, all at once, I understood. Forgetting decorum, I tore into the box eagerly, pushed aside the packing paper, and lifted my lost locket out, holding it in the air in front of me.

I was so happy I felt I might cry, and Arthur must have seen the emotion in my eyes, because he immediately began to downplay his role in the item's safe return.

"It really was no trouble. I come by this way often, anyway. I just offered to bring it by is all," he said.

"Thank you so much," I managed to say. After the day I'd had, it felt nice to have the locket back in my position, to have something tangible to tie me back to the time before India and the orphanage, before Rose or the Beckinghams ever came into my life. To tie me back to New York. And to Jimmy. "Where did you find it?"

"Near the docks," he answered a little too quickly. The answer felt prepared, and confusing. I had been in the alley behind the jazz club when I'd lost my necklace. The docks were close to the club, sure, but that still wouldn't explain how my locket would have travelled two blocks away by itself.

I pursed my lips. "It's funny how lost items can travel without you," I said.

His eyes narrowed slightly. "Yes, it certainly is."

"I'm amazed you noticed such a small locket. And grateful that you moved to return it. Most people would have kept it for themselves, or, in the case of this old thing, thrown it away," I joked. "I know the necklace would have little value to anyone else, but it has a great deal of value to me."

"Let's hope you don't lose it again," he said.

I grabbed the locket tightly in my fist and held it to my chest. "I will be much more careful in future."

Arthur smiled politely and then half-turned towards the road, clearly eager to leave.

"I actually lost it several days ago," I said as a way to hold him there. I didn't yet understand whether fate or something more sinister had brought one of the main suspects in Frederick's murder to my doorstep, but I intended to do my best to find out. "In fact, the reason anyone knew where to return the locket is because I happened to lose it shortly before a murder occurred in the same location."

Arthur seemed much less surprised than a normal person would be at hearing such a story. He just nodded. "Are you referring to Frederick Grossmith?"

I hadn't expected him to be so forthcoming. I nodded. "Yes, the very same."

"Well, if it will ease your worries, Miss, Frederick wasn't a man anyone will be missing," he said, placing a hand alongside of his mouth as if he were telling me a secret, though there was no one around to overhear us.

"I'm not so certain his girlfriend thinks so," I said. I, of course, was referring to Everilda. I now believed her story that she and Frederick were never actually in a relationship, but it was a common belief anyway, and I wanted to see what exactly Arthur knew on the topic.

"If you're referring to Everilda, the two of them weren't a couple," he said. "If you're referring to another woman, then she's well rid of him. Frederick was no good, Miss. Let me tell you."

"Oh, so you were well acquainted with the deceased, then?"

Arthur shrugged his shoulders. "I was a regular at The Chesney Ballroom. I saw Frederick while he manned the bar. If ordering drinks from the man makes us well-acquainted, then I guess we were good pals," he joked.

"I heard Frederick had a lot of trouble with his temper. He was known to throw customers from the club, yell and shout, make a big scene." The sentence lent itself towards being a question, and Arthur understood this.

"If you're looking for someone to corroborate what you've heard, then I would be happy to oblige. Frederick and I had plenty of run-ins over the years. I wasn't his favorite customer, nor was he my favorite bartender."

"What did you argue about?" I asked.

Arthur's face flushed slightly, and he shifted his weight from foot to foot. "To be honest with you, Miss, I have a bad habit of overindulging when I drink. The wife gives me a lot of trouble for it, but I have cut back considerably. And well, Frederick didn't take too kindly to my inebriated state. He was always concerned about men bothering Everilda. But you see, I'm a married man. I wouldn't have bothered Everilda, but Frederick didn't see it that way. If I so much as looked at her, I could be thrown out to the curb."

"So, you never saw Everilda romantically?" I asked.

His eyes went wide. "Me? No, never. In fact, I often asked Everilda whether she wanted me to talk to Frederick. She made it clear she had no interest in him, but Frederick wouldn't leave her alone. He was always pushing her around and making sure every decent man in the city stayed a solid five meters away from her."

"Did she ever take you up on that offer?"

"No. No, she always insisted she could handle him. That everything was fine," he said. "I was concerned about what would happen if Frederick lost his temper with her, but she insisted she had means to take care of herself."

"Did she ever tell you what she meant by that?" I asked.

"No, and I never asked," he said. "Everilda is a tough girl, and I trusted her judgment. But as it turns out, someone else took care of him for all of us."

Encountering yet another person who showed no signs of remorse at Frederick's passing left me feeling more than a little glum. Even if the man was as terrible as everybody claimed, didn't he deserve even one nice eulogy?

"I'm sorry if I offended you," Arthur said, pulling his mouth to the side. "I suppose I seem rather crass speaking of the dead in such a way. I really ought to get going. The wife will be missing me."

I wondered whether the woman I'd seen Arthur arguing with earlier that afternoon was the one he referred to as his wife. And if she was, I wondered whether they had made up, or whether Arthur had big plans to knock on the front door of Lissa's house all evening.

"You didn't offend me," I said with a smile. "Thank you so much for finding me and returning the locket. I honestly can't express how happy it makes me to have it in my possession once again."

"Of course, Miss," Arthur said, nodding his head. "Just take care to keep it around your neck this time."

I waved as he walked down the sidewalk and turned to the right, disappearing behind the wrought iron fence cloaked in flowering ivy.

The locket bore a new scratch across the back where it had fallen and collided with the stone alley, but otherwise it looked as good as new. I flicked the locking mechanism, and released a pent up sigh when the small strip of paper fell into my open palm. Even though I knew what it would say, I used my thumb and forefinger to unfurl the piece of paper to read the two scribbled words for what had to be the thousandth time.

Help me.

I quickly rolled it back up and closed it safely inside the locket.

Then, a gunshot rang through the picturesque afternoon, and I fell to the ground.

17

I t was instinctual. The moment I heard the gunshot, I threw myself on the ground, making myself as small as possible.

A scream rang out behind me and I turned, face still pressed to the cool dirt, to see Alice standing in the doorway to the Beckingham home, her hand over her face.

"Get down, Alice," I shouted.

She obeyed, dropping to the ground, the ruffles of her dress catching on the stone steps and tearing. We both waited. My breathing came in frantic gasps and I could hear Alice softly crying behind me, but still I didn't move. I felt that perhaps the smarter thing to do would have been to run inside, but I didn't want to make myself a larger target and staying down on the ground seemed to be working. I didn't hear another gunshot. So, out of fear and indecision, I stayed put. Had Lord Ashton not come outside to see what had caused his youngest daughter to scream, I may have stayed in the face down position for the rest of my life.

"What on earth happened?" he asked, grabbing Alice's

elbow and pulling her to her feet. Alice's face was red and splotchy, wet with tears.

Lord Ashton looked over at me as though I had caused them.

"Gunfire, Uncle," I said. "Someone shot at us."

"At you?" he asked, turning to Alice, bending down in front of her to assess her injuries, which were nothing more than scraped knees.

Alice shook her head. "No, they were shooting at Rose."

"Did you see who fired that shot?" I asked, turning towards her eagerly. I'd been distracted when the gunshot rang out, and by the time I had the presence of mind to look for a shooter, my nose was already pressed into the grass.

"No, but the bullet hole is here," she said, taking a few steps towards me and pointing to a perfectly circular puncture wound in the stone face of the house. "If they were aiming for me, we can be certain they weren't a marksman."

Alice already seemed to be gaining her composure, and I was proud of the young girl for pulling herself together so quickly. Most women—and men—in her position would have been inconsolable in a similar situation. I, of course, had found myself at the wrong end of a gun before. The murderer aboard the *RMS Star of India* had attempted to shoot me moments before choosing to take his own life instead. I was no stranger to the violence guns could cause. I only felt grateful the bullet had missed its intended target and curious as to who had pulled the trigger in the first place.

Lady Ashton and Catherine came out of the house at the same time, eyes wide and panicked. Lord Ashton consoled them, and no sooner had he calmed them than Edward ran through the front gate and made directly for Alice.

"Alice, dear sister," he said, breathless, bending down in

front of his youngest sister and caressing her cherubic cheeks. "Are you harmed?"

"I am perfectly well," she said, seeming annoyed with all of the attention.

I, however, couldn't help but notice how Edward had immediately run to Alice upon arriving at the house. He hadn't even asked what had occurred to bring everyone outside and send the house into such a panic.

"Someone attempted to shoot me," I said, offering him an explanation he still hadn't asked for.

He turned to me, the concern in his eyes shifting to another emotion I couldn't place, and nodded. "Yes, several people who were walking down the road ran when they heard the gunshot. The news reached me when I was crossing the street to come back home."

"Lucky you were so close by," I said.

Edward narrowed his eyes but turned back to Alice. She was doing her best to fend off the worried hands of her mother.

"We ought to contact the police," Lord Ashton said just as on officer pushed through the front gate.

"We heard news of a gunshot from this residence?" the officer asked, eyeing each member of the family suspiciously.

Lord Ashton nodded. "That is correct, though we didn't attempt to shoot ourselves, so I suggest you expand your search beyond my property."

"We have officers scouring the neighborhood," the officer said, not bothering to hide the distain in his voice. "Countless witnesses to the event reported it and my men are on the hunt for a suspect."

"If you have witnesses, didn't they see who pulled the trigger?" I asked.

The officer shook his head and ran a hand down his weary face. "Somehow, not a single person managed to actually see a shooter. They only heard a gunshot. Are you sure you were actually shot at? It wasn't an explosion of some kind?"

I pointed to the bullet hole in the house behind me. The officer took a step closer, squinted to get a better look, and then nodded somberly. "Yes, I'm afraid that is a bullet hole. And were you the intended victim?" the officer asked, tipping his head towards me.

"I believe so," I said.

"Do you have any idea who may have wanted to shoot you?" the officer asked.

I resisted the urge to look at Edward. It still seemed suspicious to me that he had arrived so soon after the gunshot rang out and had run to Alice without a single question as to what had occurred. How had he known Alice was outside when it happened? How had he known his home was the location of the attack? There were too many questions and his story had provided few answers. Still, I didn't have grounds to accuse him. Sure, he wanted my inheritance, but would that be enough reason for him to execute me? Plus, if he did want to kill me, he had ample opportunity to do so since we were now living under the same roof. Poison would be a much less obvious, less suspicious way to achieve the same ends. A shiver ran down my spine as I thought of how easily Edward could be rid of me if he so desired.

Then, my mind flicked to Arthur Burton. He had been gone less than a minute when the shot rang out. He was my main suspect in Frederick Grossmith's murder, he had arrived at my doorstep with my missing locket, and it was possible he had recognized me from outside of his house earlier that afternoon. Perhaps he discovered I was the "witness" to Frederick's murder, and seeing me outside of his house led him to believe I was on his trail. Perhaps he wanted to do away with me before I could turn him in. Before I could identify him as the shooter. Of course, I knew I couldn't identify anyone as the shooter since I had neither seen nor heard Frederick being shot, but there was a good chance Arthur didn't know that.

"If I knew someone who wanted to shoot me, I wouldn't be standing exposed in front of my house," I said to the officer as kindly as I could.

He tightened his lips and nodded, clearly tired of dealing with citizens for the day.

"We will alert you if we discover anything," he said. "Please, go inside and stay there for the evening. Police presence will be heavy in this area for the next few days until we are able to determine what exactly happened here."

Lord and Lady Ashton thanked the officer as he left, and then grumbled all the way through dinner about the police's inability to nab a suspect. Edward, who had arrived home beside himself with worry, grew steadily quieter as the evening dragged on. His brows drew together in thought, and he barely touched his dinner. Alice, who had at first been annoyed by the attention she was receiving, began to miss it as everyone's attention switched to other topics. Her memory of the incident became more vivid and elaborate with each retelling. Catherine seemed incapable of doing anything other than casting her gaze nervously between her brother and me, no doubt trying to decide how she could repair the damaged relationship she believed to be her own doing.

Dinner was exhausting. I ate my food and quietly excused myself before dessert. Adrenaline alone had carried me through the questioning by police and the beginning of dinner, but by the end, my head was drooping and I desperately needed the comfort and solitude of my bed. When my head finally hit the pillow, the reality of the situation crashed over me.

I'd almost been murdered.

Again.

For the third time in as many months, someone had made an attempt on my life. First, the explosion in Simla that killed the Beckinghams. Second, when Dr. Rushforth attempted to strangle me on the ship once I suspected him as the killer. And now, third, the mystery shooter.

Did the attack have something to do with Frederick Grossmith's murder? Had I once again come too close to solving the case and put my own life in jeopardy? Or had it been a member of my own family? Had Edward attempted to take my life to ensure my inheritance went to him? If Catherine was to be believed, the Beckinghams were not in a financially secure situation, and my fortune would certainly solve the brunt of their issues.

The question of who pulled the trigger stayed at the forefront of my mind, inhibiting rest until my body could no longer fight it off and I sunk into a fitful sleep full of shadowy attackers and the sound of gunfire.

18

A side from Alice's incessant discussion of the shooting and the miraculous way she had dodged the bullet by throwing herself to the ground at the last possible moment, Ashton House seemed to have settled back into its normal routine by the next morning. No one seemed overly concerned with the shooting or what it meant for the safety of the family. In fact, Lord Ashton had decided, apparently overnight, that the bullet that had lodged itself in the stone façade of his home must have been a stray bullet shot from the gun of a "passing troublemaker." His wife, eager to rid herself of the excitement from the day before, latched onto this theory, as well.

I wanted to dissuade them from becoming comfortable so quickly after the shooting, for fear another attack would be made, but I was no closer to answering the question of who pulled the trigger than the police were. The sergeant had come by the house during breakfast to inform Lord Ashton that his officers had walked themselves weary the night before and found nothing of any consequence.

"I would not pull my men from your neighborhood if I

believed you or any member of your family could be in danger," the man said, his voice floating from the entrance hall into the dining room where myself and the rest of the Beckingham family sat still as statues, unchewed food sitting on our tongues lest we chew and miss a single word. "It's just that this neighborhood is exceptionally safe, and my men are needed in other areas of the city."

"Of course," Lord Ashton said. I could picture him puffing out his chest in an effort to make himself seem larger, more intimidating. "Thank you for all you have done for my family."

All they'd done? I couldn't see how walking around a neighborhood all evening was much of anything. Of course, I hadn't told anyone in the family or any of the questioning officers that I was looking into the murder of Frederick Grossmith, but they did know I was a witness to the crime, which should have sparked some kind of connection between the two investigations. Frederick Grossmith was killed with a gun and then someone shot at the only possible witness a few days later? That seemed a bit too coincidental for a stray bullet. Whether it was the murderer or Edward seeking to make it look as though I were killed because of what I'd seen the day I arrived in London, I couldn't be certain. But the only thing I did know for sure was that the bullet was intended for me, and whoever fired it wouldn't hesitate to do so again.

If Achilles Prideaux hadn't refused to assist me unless I spilled all of my secrets to him, I would have called him to ask for his opinion on the case. Of course, perhaps if he knew my life was in danger, he would be more willing to help me.

"Now life can get back to normal," Lord Ashton declared as he reclaimed his seat at the breakfast table. He took a deep breath and then released the air from his lungs, as if purging himself of the stress brought on by the previous night's activity.

"The sergeant isn't worried about another incident?" Lady Ashton asked, saying the word 'incident' in a hushed tone.

I couldn't understand why everyone seemed ashamed, as if they themselves had fired the bullet and wished for no one to find out. In my estimation, we were the victims and shouldn't have any shame on the subject at all. However, not wishing to make anyone more uncomfortable than neces- sary, I had kept discussion of the shooting to a minimum. Alice, on the other hand...

"Does he think someone will try to shoot us again?" she asked boldly, interrupting her parents' discussion.

Lord Ashton took a sip of his tea and pursed his lips. "No, there will be no repeat of last night. He believes it was an accident and I agree."

Alice opened her mouth to argue, but Edward reached over and patted his younger sister's hand. She looked up at him, eyebrows furrowed, but she couldn't maintain her serious face when he winked at her. Alice returned the wink and then smiled conspiratorially as she hovered over her breakfast.

I, however, nearly fell out of my chair at the sight of Edward doing anything but scowling and looking morose. When had he become so brotherly? So caring? I was still trying to determine whether he was always serious or whether that was something he reserved only for me. Perhaps, he was always this kind to Alice and I just hadn't had occasion to see it before. Or maybe he was riddled with guilt for nearly shooting his own sister in an attempt to shoot me.

I knew it was a far-fetched theory, but I also couldn't shake the idea from my mind. Catherine had confessed to me the very day of the shooting that Edward believed me to be an imposter. She said he had his sights set on my inheritance, and he had been less than pleased to learn I had survived the explosion. Was that not motive enough?

As I watched Edward dote on his sister, he shifted his attention to me. I quickly looked away, staring at the condensation rolling down the pitcher of milk near my plate, but I could feel Edward's dark eyes on me. His gaze was heavy, like a warm blanket on a hot day, suffocating.

When breakfast ended, I excused myself immediately, planning to go into the back garden. If Edward was the shooter, he wouldn't attempt such a feat again—not when everyone's attention was piqued. And if Edward wasn't the shooter, perhaps the real villain would try again and, if they once again missed their mark, I would get a good look at them.

"Do you think it is a good morning for a walk?" Lady Ashton asked, casting her nervous eyes from me to the window. It was clear she was more uneasy about the shooting than she wanted to let on.

"The weather is fine, and there is a lovely breeze moving through the trees," I said with a smile. "It feels like a sin to be indoors."

She gave me a shaky nod and looked to her husband to discourage me further, but he was lost in his newspaper and showed no concern at all as I left the house.

I tried not to look at the bullet hole marring the front of the Beckingham's home. Seeing it brought up a surge of emotions I wasn't ready to dissect. I moved past it, keeping my eyes resolutely forward, and by my third lap around the house I was almost able to forget about it entirely. The day truly was lovely. People moved up and down the street, tipping their hats to those they passed, smiling as they gazed up through the lacework of leaves and tree branches to the unusually blue sky above. I was almost able to forget about the events of the previous day entirely. Almost.

As I rounded the front of the house for my fourth pass through the front garden, I spotted a figure out of the corner of my eye. My body, still riddled with anxieties lurking just below the surface, shot to attention. I jumped backwards and threw myself against the stone wall, flattening myself to become as small of a target as possible.

I stood there, breathing heavily, my heart leaping against my ribcage, when I realized nothing was happening. No sound, no movement. After a few deep breaths, I stepped forward and poked my head timidly around the stone corner. The figure was gone.

My head tilted to the side as I tried to determine whether I'd imagined the figure or whether it had actually been there. A young couple moved down the path in front of Ashton House, seemingly without a care. Certainly, if they'd seen a gunman lurking in the bushes they would have raised the alarm. Perhaps, I had imagined it.

Doing my best to move casually, I strode across the front garden and followed the stone path through the wrought iron gate that opened onto the street. I was prepared to chalk the entire thing up to nerves. As much as I wanted to try and forget it, being shot at had left me feeling jangled. However, before I could convince myself to turn around and go back inside the gate I caught something just at the edge of my vision. Near the end of the block, I saw him. George.

I'd nearly missed him because he was stooped over, the top half of his body practically buried in the hedge, but he'd come up for air just as I was beginning to turn back towards the house. I ducked back behind the coverage of the bush and watched. George seemed to be looking for something, and it took me a few seconds to realize he was standing in exactly the same place where I believed the gunman to have stood.

George righted himself and glanced around to see whether anyone had noticed his odd behavior. Miraculously, no one else seemed to find it strange at all, and George was free to move on down the block, away from the Beckingham's home.

I knew I could go back inside and report his behavior to Lord and Lady Ashton. However, telling them about George snooping through the bush would mean nothing to them unless I also told them about his past. About his run in with the dead man at the docks. About how I'd seen blood on the door handle the morning Frederick was killed and found the burnt remains of George's driving gloves. It would almost certainly lead to him being fired from his chauffeur position whether he was guilty of killing Frederick or not. And even with all of that evidence, I still wasn't certain George had done it. If he had wanted to kill me, he could have done so when he found me breaking into his room. So, it didn't seem to make any sense for him to wait and try to shoot me later, especially when I had moved on to other suspects. No, I needed more evidence.

I stepped away from the bush and followed George down the street, keeping a fair amount of distance between us so that even if he saw me, it wouldn't be obvious I had been following him. When he turned the corner at the end of the block, though, I broke into a run so as not to lose him. The heels of my shoes slapped against the concrete, so I shifted onto my toes, and all of the passersby who didn't pay any mind while a grown man dug through a hedge were suddenly gawking at me as though I were a zany street performer.

I reached the corner just in time to see George duck down the alley that ran behind Ashton House. My breathing was already erratic from running, but I pushed on, hustling to the mouth of the alley before George could disappear. As soon as I had him in my sights again, I slowed down to a normal pace, trying to let my ragged breathing return to normal. If George did wish to kill me and he spotted me following him, I wouldn't have the energy to run away. I would have to roll over and depend on his mercy, because it felt as though my lungs were going to burst.

When George turned sharply to the right and disappeared behind a fence I groaned and hung my head, not at all prepared to chase after him yet again. However, a few more steps revealed that he had gone into the Beckingham's back garden. He had taken a rather circuitous route, especially since he could have just come through the front gate and walked around the back of the house. Unless, of course, the Beckinghams didn't want the help using the front entrance?

Had I been following George for absolutely no reason? Had I nearly fainted in the street due to lack of oxygen because George had to walk back to his room?

I felt silly. Clearly, the investigation was going to my head. I was beginning to see suspicious behavior where there was only daily routine. However, I decided my running would not be in vain. I remembered a window along the back wall of George's room when I'd broken in the first time, so when George unlocked his front door and stepped inside, I sneaked around the back of the building.

It took me a minute or two to gather the courage to peek my head over the window sill. I kept imagining George standing just on the other side of the window, staring at me as I stood up, a gun held in his hand. However, as I looked through the window I didn't see George at all. Somehow, that left an even larger knot in my stomach. Where had he gone? Just as I was growing bold, leaning closer to the glass and peering into every corner of the room, George came into view. He walked out of a washroom in the back corner and luckily, he was too engrossed to notice me at the window. I ducked down immediately, heart hammering as if I'd just run another few city blocks.

Slowly, I lifted back up to watch him. He was standing in the middle of the room, mesmerized by something in his hands. It appeared to be some kind of fabric—a handkerchief or a bit of cloth—and he rubbed it between his fingers. His eyebrows were pulled together in deep thought, and I had the feeling I could have rapped my knuckles on the glass and it wouldn't have disturbed him.

George reached behind him to pull the cord of a lamp, illuminating the dark room, and consequently, the fabric in his hands.

Now that I could see it properly, I realized it was not a handkerchief at all. The fabric was ripped along one of the edges as though it had been torn from a larger garment, and it was intricately adorned with beads that caught the light from the lamp as George moved the material through his fingers. Suddenly, I was struck with a memory.

I ducked below the window and pressed my spine against the wall, my eyes shifting constantly but seeing nothing. I was too busy searching my mind, shifting through my memories to find where I'd seen that material before, until I had it.

Everilda Cassel.

The fabric came from the dress I'd seen Everilda

wearing the first night I'd gone to The Chesney Ballroom. George had told me he didn't even remember Everilda's name. He'd claimed the fight between him and Frederick did not stem from any feelings George had for Everilda, but purely from Frederick's jealousy. But, if that were true, why did George have a bit of her dress?

The truth hit me all at once. George loved Everilda. He loved her and Frederick had decided to stand in his way. Frederick laid claim to Everilda, and George killed him because of it. It was the only thing that made sense.

After all, Everilda had recognized George by name when I mentioned him to her. She remembered him coming in regularly for a drink. Whereas, George swore he didn't know her at all. Why would he go so far as to claim he didn't know her name? Any patron of The Chesney Ballroom would know Everilda's name. It was announced on the microphone before each of her performances.

I slipped away from George's place and moved quickly down the alley towards the street. I knew it would be wise to go to the police. I could tell them what I knew, everything I'd uncovered in my investigation. And I would, just not yet. First, I wanted to talk to Everilda. I needed to warn her about George, allow her to protect herself.

The lovely day felt suddenly more dreary as I navigated the London streets towards The Chesney Ballroom.

19

My legs were fatigued and my brain felt fuzzy with exhaustion, but purpose propelled me onward. I would have hailed a cab, but I left the Beckingham's in such a hurry that I didn't have any money on hand. So, I was left to walk the entire way to the jazz club. I found myself grateful for the extra time to plan what I was going to say to Everilda. I didn't want to scare her unnecessarily, but it only seemed right that she should know about George's feelings and about what he had likely done to Frederick. Again, the urge to go to the police was strong, but I knew how the law worked. Slowly. Who knew what damage George could get done in the time it would take for officers to arrest him? I decided to tell Everilda and then walk directly to the station.

Just as I had on the ship from India to London, I found myself wondering how I could have let such evil slip by unnoticed. First, Dr. Rushforth had fooled me entirely, making me believe he was a friend even though he had killed poor Ruby Stratton. And now, George. His story had fooled me utterly. I had never fully let go of him as a suspect, but he had certainly moved to the end of a rather long line. Was it so easy to trick me? George's sob story had given me pause. I hadn't wanted to be responsible for a good man losing his job, so I'd sat on the information I had when I should have been turning him in to the police. Briefly, I imagined how I would have felt if George had managed to kill Alice when he fired the gun at me. If my baby cousin had died because I'd kept evidence from the police. A shudder tore through me. The thought was too horrible to entertain. Thankfully, my foolish error seemed to have caused no one any serious harm. There was still time to make things right.

The lovely breeze from that morning had shifted into a proper gale, lifting the skirt of my cream tea dress. I pulled my navy sweater tighter over my shoulders and lowered my head against the chill. I was only a few blocks away from The Jazz Club, and perhaps Everilda would be so grateful for the warning, she would pay for my cab to the police station. I wouldn't ask for money, of course, but perhaps if I mentioned the chill...

I was only a few buildings away from The Chesney Ballroom when the sound of heels against concrete caught my attention and I looked up to see a woman in black oxfords and a shin-length black dress moving in front of me. Her steps were quick and determined, and I looked around, trying to decide where she'd come from. I'd been mostly alone on the street only a moment before. I looked back at the woman, puzzled, and realized all at once who I was looking at.

Her long, lean arms hanging from the loose sleeves of her dress. Her short curly hair slicked back against her head.

"Everilda," I called, quickening my pace to catch up to her.

She turned, looking hardly surprised to see me, and smiled. "Rose, isn't it?"

I nodded quickly and immediately began to launch into the story, the words tumbling out of me in a jumble. Everilda's smile faded as I spoke and she glanced around the empty street, clearly concerned about who could overhear. She held up a hand to silence me, and I swallowed the storm of unspoken words, nearly choking on them.

"Follow me," she whispered, her thin brows pulled together. She reached for my hand and I let her pull me down the street in the direction of the club. However, just as the front doors of The Chesney came into view, Everilda took a hard right into the building next door.

"Where are we going?" I asked as Everilda pushed open the creaky front doors and stepped into the dark space. The light from the street illuminated a snowstorm of dust in the air. It was obvious the building had been in disuse for quite a long period of time.

"Tom owns this building, too," Everilda said, letting go of my hand, but still ushering me inside.

I hesitated in the doorway. "Why can't we just go into the club?"

"Everyone in the club has been given explicit orders not to discuss Frederick's murder. Tom says it is bad for business. I don't want him to hear me talking about it with a customer and lose my job," she said.

"Would he really dismiss you for talking to me?" I asked, taking a few tentative steps inside, clearing the doorway.

Everilda nodded. "Especially for talking to you. You've got a reputation for asking a lot of questions." She offered a reassuring smile, her teeth glinting for a moment before she closed the door and plunged us both into darkness.

"Are there any lights in here?" I asked.

"None that work. Tom bought this place when it went up for sale a few years ago hoping to expand the club into this building, but he never got around to it. Now it just sits here empty. I sometimes come in here to take my breaks."

I tried to imagine Everilda—luminous, glamorous Everilda—sitting in this dark, dusty space. Somewhere in the depths of the building I could hear water dripping in a constant rhythm. The wind from outside whistled through the cracks in the walls and around the grimy windows. I couldn't understand why she'd rather be in here than in her dressing room, but there were more important things to consider.

"I came to speak with you," I said, beginning the conversation in a much calmer, more rational manner than I had the first time.

Everilda laughed. "I gathered that from your tirade on the street. This has something to do with Frederick?"

"Yes. Frederick and you. I believe you may be in danger," I said.

She reared back, head tilted. "How so?"

"I believe the man you were speaking to the night before Frederick's murder, George Hoskins, is Frederick's killer."

"What evidence do you have?" she asked calmly.

I explained the blood on the door handle, the burnt gloves, and what I'd seen that very morning. "He was caressing a scrap of your dress between his fingers, staring at it as though it were the most important thing in the world," I said.

"He had a piece of my dress? The gold one?"

I nodded, and Everilda turned away from me, pacing

into the shadows of the building, running her hands down her body as though checking to make sure all of her limbs were present. Then, she turned back to me, smiling.

"I don't see what there is to smile about," I said truthfully. "This man is clearly deranged and you are the object of his delusions. I only wanted to warn you of his feelings before going to the police. It seemed like the right thing to do. I do hope you will take the necessary precautions to protect yourself and others from him. If he was willing to kill Frederick, he may very well be willing to kill any man who dares to stand between the two of you being together."

"Taking care of myself has never been an issue for me," Everilda said, tilting her head to the side, looking me up and down, assessing me.

Suddenly, I realized how little I knew Everilda. I'd spoken to her once, but otherwise we were perfect strangers. I hadn't told anyone where I was going. In fact, it was unlikely anyone in the Beckingham household had even realized I was gone.

"Well," I said, nodding my head slowly, "Good. I hope the police will apprehend George and he will be no further trouble to you, but I thought it best if I delivered the news to you first."

Everilda moved towards me, nodding. "Yes, that was definitely best. I do appreciate it so much. I can hardly tell you."

She brushed my shoulder and then moved past me, standing between me and the front door. I couldn't say why exactly, but I took a step backwards, wanting to put space between myself and Everilda. Perhaps it was her smile. The way her lips barely moved, yet her entire face glowed with something cheerfully menacing. Her eyes were wide and half-crazed. I began to wonder whether I shouldn't have warned George about Everilda. *No sense killing anyone over her. She's loony.*

"I ought to get going now," I said, the words sticking in my throat.

Everilda shook her head. "I don't think you'll be going anywhere, unfortunately."

Then, the hand I hadn't realized was behind her back came into view, a silver gun clutched in her painted nails. She must have withdrawn it from her purse earlier.

I wanted to gasp in shock, stumble backwards in surprise. But I couldn't. Somehow, the moment she'd pulled me into the abandoned building, I'd known something was off. I couldn't say I'd expected it, because if I had, I would be insane to have followed her. But something about the interaction had left me uneasy. I'd chalked it up to the excitement of the morning and nerves about telling Everilda the truth about Frederick, but now I knew it had been my survival instincts prickling, begging me to stay in the sunlight.

Her wide eyes narrowed as she looked at me, the gun blocking my view of her lips. "You do not seem surprised, Rose," she said.

"Sorry to disappoint you." My heart had climbed into my throat and with every passing second, panic seeped into my arms and legs. I felt cemented in place, unable to move. While my body stood frozen, my mind whirled, rearranging the evidence into a different picture. Everilda had made it clear she didn't want to lose her job, and Frederick's possessiveness was a threat to her position. She had been welcoming to me the first time we'd spoken, but she had practically shunned me when she saw me lurking around The Chesney Ballroom again. And the dress. I'd seen George holding a piece of her dress, but I'd also seem him digging in the bush just outside the Beckingham's house moments before. I'd assumed he had taken it from her in the past as a token, but he had actually found it in the bush. Her dress had likely caught on one of the branches of the shrubbery when she'd fired her gun at me and then run off to blend in with the panicked crowd on the street. George had probably only picked the fabric up to puzzle over the clue. I had made too many incorrect assumptions.

Everilda let the gun fall to her side. "You haven't disappointed me. Far from it. You've been a good little detective. Much more impressive than the police. Unfortunately, it seems you came to the wrong conclusion."

"Then why reveal yourself?" I asked, voice strong despite my trembling fingers. No matter how many times I found myself on the bullet end of a gun, the sense of panic and terror never went away. "I had pinned the crime on the wrong man."

"But for how long?" Everilda asked, shrugging her thin shoulders. "You have been relentless. It was only a matter of time before you discovered the truth. And, if not you, then the police certainly would have pieced it together eventually. Granted, I could have packed up and run away, started over somewhere else, but I'm tired of running and hiding. I like working at The Chesney, and I refuse to let Frederick or anyone else ruin it for me, you included."

"How was Frederick ruining things for you?" I asked, genuinely curious, though I also knew my best chance at survival rested on my ability to keep Everilda talking. If she was talking, she wasn't pulling the trigger.

Everilda groaned, her painted lips pursing in annoyance. "Speaking of being relentless," she said, using the gun to gesture at me and rolling her eyes. "Frederick insisted we were a couple. He helped make the schedules and he always scheduled us to work together so he knew all of my days off. He would show up at my house to walk me to work, wait for me outside of the club so he could walk me home, and he practically assaulted any man who even looked at me."

Everilda paced back and forth in front of the door, the gun dangling at her side like a cold metal accessory. "Tom made it clear when he hired me that he wouldn't stand for romantic relationships between his employees, and I agreed. But Frederick didn't give me a choice, and with the way he was behaving, it wouldn't have been long before Tom found out and fired us both."

"Why didn't you just tell Tom what was going on?" I asked. "You could have told him Frederick was pursuing you, but you were not interested. He wouldn't fire you over another employee's indiscretion, surely."

She stopped pacing for a moment and looked at me, one eyebrow raised in clear disbelief at my naiveté. "Do you believe I would be in this situation if the solution was that simple? Do you think I would have killed Frederick if there was any other way?"

I opened my mouth and then closed it, unsure what to say. I found it hard to believe killing someone could be the only plausible solution to a problem, but it seemed reckless to say something like that to Everilda, especially while she was holding the gun.

"When we first spoke, I told you Frederick liked to blackmail people," she said, her annoyance falling into a defeated exhaustion.

"He was blackmailing you?" I asked.

She nodded but didn't move to say anything else. I hesitated, unsure whether it was wise to push her to say more. However, if she decided to stop talking now, I knew it wouldn't be long before she decided to start shooting.

"What information did he have on you?"

"I made a few poor decisions," she began with a sigh.

I wanted to feign shock. *Everilda make a poor decision? The woman threatening to murder me? Surely not.* Thankfully, I bit my tongue and let her continue.

"Singing at The Chesney Ballroom is everything to me. It's how I support myself and it is the only way I make money. But, I still struggle. I confided in Frederick not long after I started that I would need to find a better paying job eventually, and he let me in on his secret."

Everilda hesitated for dramatic effect and I held my breath, waiting.

"He swore me to secrecy and then admitted that he had been skimming money from the club to supplement his income."

I deflated. Tom had already told me this. He had known Frederick was stealing from him and planned to fire him before he'd been murdered. If Everilda was afraid of losing her job, it could very well be too late. "Tom knows about Frederick stealing money and planned to fire him," I said, hope ballooning in my chest. "It is likely he knows about you, as well. So, there is no need to kill me."

I knew my attempt at persuasion was flimsy, but all I could do was suggest the idea and hope it stuck. If Everilda thought she would lose her job anyway, perhaps killing me would become useless. Perhaps, I would escape the abandoned building and live to see another day.

Everilda lowered her head and shook it. I didn't understand the meaning behind the gesture until she looked back up at me, a smile stretching her lips. "Frederick had been stealing money from Tom for years, and Tom only just found out. Who do you think alerted him?"

She raised an eyebrow and my hopes shattered. "You told him?"

She nodded. "I told Tom the night before...Frederick died," she said, stumbling over the inaccurate phrasing. "He thanked me for alerting him and called me a trusted member of the team. It was for added security."

I must have looked confused because she sighed and explained. "The moment I agreed to take a cut from the money Frederick was stealing, I'd unknowingly bound myself to him. He was convinced I was his and even a mumbling of discontent from me had him threatening to reveal the whole plot to Tom. Frederick had me under his thumb. The trouble was, even if he didn't tell Tom, as time went on I knew it wouldn't be long before Tom found out on his own. Frederick wasn't exactly known for his subtlety. If I told Tom about Frederick thinking we were a couple, Frederick would tell Tom about the money I'd stolen. If I stopped taking my cut of the money, then Frederick would realize I was trying to pull away from him and he'd tell Tom. I was trapped in a circle of lies and deceit and I needed to find my way out."

"Through murder," I said, my words free of judgment.

She nodded slowly. "Murder wasn't always the plan. Before Frederick, I'd never even hit another person. Violence had never been my response to problems, but then I saw the way Frederick unleashed himself on George at the bar that night. He thought George was flirting with me, and maybe he was," she said, shrugging as though she didn't care, though I noticed a flash of wistfulness in her eyes as she spoke. "Either way, Frederick lost it. He tipped over a table and spilled drinks as he stomped around the club, shouting and causing a scene. Thankfully, Tom wasn't working that night, otherwise he would have heard Frederick going on about his love for me and how he would kill George for interfering. The whole situation was unbelievable, and at that moment, the idea struck me. I could kill Frederick. His death wouldn't be a surprise to anyone who knew him. Frederick had a penchant for getting into fights regularly and biting off more than he could chew. He had come to work on more than one occasion with a swollen lip and bruised eyes. It wouldn't be too far-fetched to think he got himself into a fight that he couldn't walk away from. Once I decided on my course of action, I only had to choose my moment."

Everilda adjusted the gun in her grip, her long fingers wrapping around the handle of the gun, and I could almost see my time slipping through the neck of an hour glass. Each grain of sand representing a minute of my life, their number growing smaller and smaller as my opportunities for escape also began to shrink.

"George was thrown from the club, but Frederick couldn't let the incident go. Getting rid of George wasn't enough. He wanted to teach him a lesson. I remembered George mentioned that he would be near The Chesney Ballroom the next morning to pick someone up from the docks. If truth be told, I think George wanted me to meet him there. Instead, I passed this information along to Frederick and watched as my plan began to take shape. I knew Frederick wouldn't be able to pass up the opportunity for another altercation with George, so all I had to do was plant myself near the scene of their fight and wait for my moment. As you already know since you were present for that portion of the morning's events, the argument only lasted a few minutes and then George left, though not before giving Frederick a rightfully deserved blow to the nose. As soon as

George left, I crept out from my hiding place behind a few dumpsters."

Listening to Everilda's story brought the scene from the alley into sharp focus in my mind. I imagined myself still in the alley, seeing the events unfolding from my vantage point. Everilda moving deftly from behind a garbage can while Frederick wiped at his bleeding nose, distracted and embarrassed after his fight with George. The woman's long, lean legs stepping over the debris lying behind the club, moving ever closer to her target.

Would I have called out to warn Frederick when Everilda pulled the gun from her purse, or would I have stood there, frozen and bewitched by the events transpiring in front of me? Would I have gasped when she pulled the trigger? Screamed? Would Everilda have heard me and killed me, too?

"I think he heard me moving behind him at the very end," Everilda said, her voice distant and cold. "He tilted his head to the side to pick out where the noise was coming from, and I pulled the trigger, shooting him in the back. I didn't want him to know it was me." There was a slight tremble in her voice, the only sign that her actions had any kind of effect on her emotional state. Her eyes were round and clear, her lips relaxed and flat.

For some reason, it comforted me to know Frederick had been shot from behind. After being shot at myself, I felt it was much better to not know it was coming. Even if he was as bad as everyone said he was, no one deserved to be shot dead by the person they loved.

"The shot didn't kill him immediately, though," Everilda added after a few seconds of silence.

My breath caught in my throat, a strangled kind of cough.

"He fell to the ground, clutching at the wound that had passed through his chest as he looked up at me. I watched his features shift from shock to anger to helplessness. I watched him grapple to understand why I had a gun in my hand, why his chest hurt so badly, why he was finding it difficult to breathe. And then, I watched as the pool of blood around him grew larger and his skin went pale. I watched him die."

My skin prickled with fear and adrenaline. Everilda would kill me. I understood that now. In the first moment I saw her with the gun, there had been a thought in the back of my head that she wouldn't be able to do it. That I would be able to talk her down. Looking in her eyes now, though, I saw the truth. She would kill me as surely as she'd killed Frederick. She would watch me die and then go to work, singing songs for the customers in the club who had no idea the horrors she had wrought in the abandoned building next door.

I steeled myself for the fight. I wouldn't go easily. Not the way Frederick had. Everilda wouldn't surprise me. My eyes were wide open, and I was ready for whatever would come next.

20

"You had a good plan, Everilda," I said, breaking the silence that had fallen over us and pulling Everilda from the memories of the fateful morning she killed Frederick. "All signs pointed to George. He had a motive and was present at the crime scene. It was a very good plan."

She looked up at me, a darkness in her eyes. "Not good enough, apparently. You were about to unravel it, which is why I had to discover where you lived and take that shot at you in front of your fancy house."

I shrugged, trying my best to hide the nervous trembles moving up my body. "This isn't my first time solving a mystery," I said by way of explanation. "And I have a good many secrets of my own. Perhaps that makes it easier for me to see through other's lies."

I hoped my vague hint at secrets would intrigue Everilda. I needed more time to plan my escape. There was a set of metal stairs at the back of the warehouse that disappeared upward toward the ceiling, and though I would have rather run out the front door and onto the street, the stairs seemed like a safer bet. She was firmly guarding the door and I didn't want to move any closer to the gun than I currently was. I only needed to distract her long enough to move a bit closer to the stairs.

"You don't seem like the type who would have any secrets," she said, practically rolling her eyes. "The night we met, I noticed you dancing with a stiff-necked man who seemed to think he was superior to everyone and everything in the club. Those types of people have very uninteresting lives, in my experience."

"I agree. *Those people* do tend to be a little dull," I said.

She raised an eyebrow at me. "Are you trying to say you are not one of those people?"

I shook my head and leaned in slightly, whispering even though we were completely alone. "My name is not Rose, and I am certainly not a Beckingham."

Everilda leaned back and lifted her chin, her eyes narrowed at me. "What do you mean?"

"I'm impersonating a dead heiress in order to obtain her inheritance money," I said coldly, trying to match Everilda's own callous demeanor. I wanted her to think we were the same—two women trying to look out for ourselves.

Her lips parted in surprise, though she quickly rebounded, adjusting her grip on the gun and then crossing her arms. "How did you manage such a thing as that?"

Once again, I was grateful for my interesting life story. It had saved me aboard the *RMS Star of India* when I used my tale to distract Dr. Rushforth as he attempted to kill me, and I only hoped it would be enough to save me now.

"I worked as a servant and companion to a Miss Rose Beckingham while she and her family lived abroad in India," I said, speaking slowly and beginning to pace back and forth. "A couple months ago, she and her family were killed in a car explosion that I narrowly survived."

"Is that how you acquired the scar on your cheek?" she asked, using the hand holding the gun to gesture towards my face.

I did my best not to flinch and nodded, my own hand absentmindedly caressing the dented bone. "Yes. I was lucky to escape with only the scar. I was also lucky to bear a striking resemblance to Rose, who was made unrecognizable by the blast." A sob thickened the walls of my throat, but I fought it back. I couldn't show any weakness. I swallowed and turned on my heels, continuing my pace. With every small lap, I shifted ever so slightly towards the back wall and the staircase. I hoped the movement was subtle enough that Everilda did not notice. "I easily passed for Rose Beckingham and made my way from India to London to claim my inheritance."

"What do you intend to do with the inheritance? It must be very important for you to risk coming here and being found out by her family," Everilda said.

I nodded. "I plan to use the money to locate a missing person. My brother Jimmy disappeared many years ago, and I hope to find him and then solve another old mystery that has plagued my family."

I took several steps and then pivoted, sliding closer to the stairs, and then pacing back in the other direction. Everilda's eyes were wide and eager. She was enraptured by my tale.

I continued. "When I was a young girl, my parents were the victims of a double murder in our New York slum. My brother, only a teenager at the time, disappeared on the same day. No one was ever charged with the crime, and the police believed my brother's disappearance to be a sign of his guilt."

Chancing a look back at the stairs, I was much closer than I had been at the beginning of my story. It would only take a few more paces for me to be close enough to make a run for the stairs and hopefully be able to make it safely up them before Everilda had time to fire her gun.

"What do you think happened to your brother if he did not commit the crime?" Everilda asked.

I shrugged. "He could have discovered the bodies of our parents and then run away in fear, staying away once he became an official police suspect. Or, perhaps, he saw the killer and then was too terrified to come forward. Either way, I need to find him and uncover the truth, which can only be done with Rose Beckingham's inheritance funding my search."

Even though telling the story had been a ploy to distract my attempted shooter, it felt surprisingly good to unburden myself. The secret had weighed heavily on my shoulders for weeks, and I relished the opportunity to reveal my plan to someone. Even if that someone still wanted to kill me.

Everilda shook her head in disbelief, a small smiling spreading across her face. "You lead a very interesting life, indeed, *Rose*." She said my assumed name with a knowing look, and for a brief second, it felt like we were old friends swapping secrets. I wondered whether my reveal wouldn't indebt us to one another. A secret for a secret.

"Unfortunately," Everilda continued, dashing all hopes of a truce between us, "I still cannot let you leave here today."

"But I understand why you did what you did," I said. "Frederick blackmailed you and fooled you. He was possessive and abusive. He gave you no other choice."

I did not believe Everilda had been forced into her decision, but now was not the time for honesty. The sand in my hourglass was nearing its end, and I had to do everything in my power to save myself.

"Your understanding will make it a bit harder to kill you," Everilda said with a slight shoulder shrug. Then, she lifted the gun in front of her, both arms straightened so the barrel was aimed at my chest. "However, I will do my best."

I dove sideways just as the shot rang out, the metal bullet striking the brick wall behind where I'd stood, sending dust everywhere. Not wasting a second, I propelled myself towards the stairs, kicking off my heeled shoes as I ran to move even more quickly. The cold metal stairs bit into the bottoms of my feet, but I barely felt it. Everilda roared in frustration below me, every sound echoing through the empty building, making it sound as though I was being chased by countless gunmen. Or gunwomen.

I didn't turn around to see where she was because I could feel the vibration of her moving up the stairs behind me. I hunched forward as I ran, trying to make myself as small of a target as possible.

When I reached the top of the staircase, I noticed a door set into the far wall, and I ran for it with abandon. If I could get to the roof, I could scream for help and try to attract attention from the street below. Perhaps, if Everilda knew she would never get away with her crime, she wouldn't shoot me.

Everilda reached the top of the staircase when I was only halfway across the room, and another shot blew a hole in the brick next to the door, letting in a smoking circle of daylight. My legs felt heavy and my bare feet were sliced and bleeding from the construction debris on the floor, but I pushed on. If I didn't get outside, I wouldn't survive. It was as simple as that.

I threw my entire weight into the door and the immobile slab of wood knocked the wind out of me. I stumbled backwards and it took me a few seconds to realize I needed to pull the door open, not push. Trying to make up the precious seconds I'd lost, I scrambled for the handle and flung the door open, stepping out onto the roof next to that of The Chesney Ballroom. Daylight blinded me, and I blinked against the sun. I wanted to keep running, but sensed I was already near the edge of the building and didn't want to accidentally run off the side. I knew I was losing time, but I only hoped Everilda would be as disoriented as I was when she reached the roof.

Just as my vision began to come back, I heard the door behind me slam shut and then I was on the ground.

Everilda's heaving chest was pressed into my spine, her hot breath against my neck. "Make a sound and I'll kill you," she hissed. It must have been an instinctive threat, because it was far too late to worry about making noise now.

I rolled underneath her, and she stood up, her feet positioned on either side of my hips, the gun pointed at my face. The sun beamed behind her, silhouetting her so that she was nothing more than a dark outline.

"You don't have to do this," I said.

"I've already killed once," Everilda said, her shadowy shoulders shrugging as if taking my life were of little consequence. "Whether I'm charged with Frederick's murder or yours and Frederick's, the sentence will be the same. I'll be hanged. And killing you is my best chance of not being charged at all."

I opened my mouth to say something, but Everilda's

fingers moved over the trigger and there was a deafening bang.

I was certain I'd been shot and I squeezed my eyes shut, waiting for the pain to consume me. Instead, I heard a scream and felt Everilda's legs stumbling over my mid-section. I opened my eyes and saw her looking back towards the door, the gun swinging wildly in her hands. I followed her gaze and thought for sure I'd been shot, the blood loss causing hallucinations. Edward stood in the doorway, his shoulders broad, eyes alert and searching.

Everilda had been momentarily stunned by his arrival, causing her to fire the gun and miss, but she was rebounding quickly. If my math was correct, she had two bullets left in the gun, which was more than enough for her to kill both of us and escape. Just as she raised her arms to aim for Edward, I kicked my legs out to the side. Luckily, she was still within reach of me and my feet collided with her knees. She screamed and pulled the trigger, a shot ringing out just as she lost her balance and tumbled over the side of the building.

21

I stared, open-mouthed, at the place where just a few moments before Everilda had been standing. My body didn't believe she was gone. Despite having witnessed her fall over the side, I kept waiting for her to return and take another shot.

"Are you all right, Rose?" Edward asked, kneeling down next to me, his hands moving across my shoulders and down my arms, assessing me.

I looked at him and then back to where Everilda had fallen over the edge. Edward followed my gaze and moved quickly to the ledge. When he looked over the side, he winced.

"She's dead," he said, turning back to me.

We didn't speak as Edward helped me to my feet and led me back into the warehouse. It felt as though I was stumbling through a dream. Or a nightmare. It wasn't until we were at the front door, only a few feet away from stepping onto the street, that I stopped.

"How did you find me?"

Edward seemed eager to leave the building, but he

stopped and faced me. "I saw you behind the house looking in on George in his flat, and then I saw you take off down the alley. Whatever you were doing seemed urgent."

"You followed me?" I asked.

"Aren't you glad I did?" he responded.

I didn't answer. Of course, I was glad. He'd saved me. But now I had to wonder how much he'd overheard. Did he hear my confession to Everilda? Did he know I was lying about my identity?

"I lost sight of you on the street and was about to step into The Chesney Ballroom to look for you when I heard the first gunshot. I came inside just as you reached the top of the stairs."

If he didn't come in until after the gunshot, then it was unlikely he'd heard any of my confession. And if he had, I supposed it was unlikely he would have bothered risking his life to save me.

"Why were you spying on George?" he asked, interrupting my thoughts.

I explained everything to him—how I had suspected George from the beginning and had been investigating the murder to try and rule him out. I explained why I went to The Chesney Ballroom in the first place and how I'd met Everilda. I told him that she was the person who had tried to shoot me the day before. And when I finished, Edward only nodded for a few seconds.

"So, George has a criminal past?" he asked, finally breaking the silence.

I nodded, head low. "I should have told you all as soon as I suspected him, but he swore he hadn't committed the murder and he didn't want to lose his position with your family. And now that Everilda confessed, I know he was telling the truth. Please don't tell your parents about him," I begged. "I truly believe he is a good man."

Edward studied me for a few seconds and then clasped a hand on my shoulder. "We need to get to the police station."

He pushed open the front door and we stepped out onto the street together. I could see a crowd gathering around where Everilda had fallen and I looked away quickly, not wanting to see. I'd seen enough human carnage in my lifetime. Unexpectedly, a sob rose in my throat.

The day had been an emotional rollercoaster. I'd come to warn Everilda of danger, and unknowingly stepped into it myself. Once again, I had nearly lost my life at the hands of a murderer.

"Are you all right?" Edward asked again, echoing what he'd asked on the roof.

I nodded, but the quivering of my lower lip gave me away. A tear rolled down my cheek.

Edward tilted his head, studying me, and then did the most surprising thing that had happened all day. He wrapped an arm around my shoulders and pulled me into his side.

"Everything is all right now, cousin. You are safe."

Cousin. *Cousin.*

I swallowed my tears and smiled up at him. Perhaps, he was right. Maybe everything was finally all right, after all.

22

The room was large and empty, the darkness broken only by the light streaming in through the windows that dotted the far wall. My footsteps echoed against the wood floors as I inspected the place.

"How do you like it, Miss Beckingham?"

I turned to the house's current owner, a gray-haired man with a thick mustache and a kind, round face. "It's beautiful, Mr. Jacobsen."

He smiled and stepped backwards towards the door. "I will leave you to think on it for a few more minutes."

I tipped my head to him and watched him walk back outside.

The house was perfect. The neighborhood was quiet, but close enough to the heart of the city that I could walk most places. Of course, that wouldn't be much of an issue considering I would have my own driver. The Beckingham's had fired George after Edward told them about his past, despite my request to my cousin to keep the secret. It seemed Edward had grown kinder but not *that* much kinder. But I immediately offered George a position at my future home, which he readily accepted. There was a guest house out behind this place where George could live and servant's quarters behind the kitchen for Aseem. Both men had my complete trust, and I believed their shadier abilities, which made them less desirable by most employers, could be of future use to me.

I didn't anticipate being at the center of yet another murder plot anytime soon, but life had been far from predictable the last few months, so it was better to be prepared for anything.

The police didn't have any other leads, so they quickly accepted my story of Everilda's confession, and were more than content to close the case on Frederick's murder and Everilda's death. Lady Ashton gave me quite the tongue lashing for investigating yet another murder and putting myself in danger, but Lord Ashton seemed rather impressed with my gumption. Likewise, I had become a star in Alice's eyes. She wanted to talk of nothing but how I managed to escape the warehouse with my life and was very displeased that I had decided to buy a place of my own so soon after arriving in London.

However, having a place of my own seemed like a wise idea. Although everyone in the family now wholly believed me to be Rose Beckingham, having my own space would allow me to come and go freely without raising any suspicion. I would no longer need to sneak out of the house at dawn for clandestine meetings with any private investigators. Though, my only private investigator contact seemed to have gone the way of the wind. First order of business once I was settled in the new house would be to find someone else to commence the search for Jimmy.

Jimmy. It had been so long since I'd seen my brother. I reached for the locket that was now securely around my neck again and thought of the scrap of paper inside. "Help me," scribbled in Jimmy's lazy penmanship. I didn't know whether the words had been written before or after our parents' murder. And despite my belief that Jimmy was still alive, I didn't even know if that was true. He had disappeared without a trace. My only bit of confidence came from the fact that his body had not turned up bloody and mutilated the way our parents' had. If the same person who killed our parents had killed Jimmy, certainly they would have done away with him in a similarly violent manner.

No, he was out there somewhere, and he needed me. He needed to know I didn't believe he was a murderer and he needed to know someone cared about him.

A floorboard let out a long, slow creak in the room behind me, and I could tell someone was attempting to be quiet. Someone was trying to sneak up on me.

The house was mostly empty, but there was a candlestick on the mantle of the fireplace and I lunged for it, holding it in the air, ready to bring it down upon whoever sought to do me harm. I had been attacked enough times in the past several months and I wouldn't allow myself to be surprised again. Another floorboard creaked and I tightened my hold on the metal candlestick, my blood pounding in my ears.

Then, a figure peeked around the doorway into the living room where I stood and my arm relaxed, though I remained alert.

"Monsieur Prideaux?"

Achilles stepped fully into the room and glanced from me to the candlestick in my hand, his mouth quirking up into a smile. "Were you expecting someone?"

"No, but you can never be too careful." I placed the candlestick back on the mantle. "How did you find me here?"

He shrugged. "Do you forget I am a world-renowned detective, Mademoiselle Rose?"

"How could one ever forget with you constantly reminding everyone of that fact?" I smiled.

His eyebrow rose and then, despite himself, he laughed. "As you already know, I live in the neighborhood. I was out for a walk when I saw you enter this house. It was only a happy coincidence."

First Edward and now Prideaux. I was apparently much too easy to follow. I made a mental note to work on becoming more vigilant about my surroundings.

"A happy coincidence?" I asked.

"Yes, because I've been wanting to speak to you, and planned to visit Ashton House this very afternoon."

"In regards to?" I asked, letting my voice trail off.

"You came to me as a client in search of a missing person," he said.

"I recall," I said coolly, remembering the not so friendly terms under which we had parted. "If you are here for more information, I have told you already that there is nothing left for us to discuss. I do not wish to say any more, and if you cannot find Jimmy with the information I have given you, then I will have to find myself another detective."

"I recall," he said, smiling as he repeated my own response back to me.

"Then, why are you here?" I asked.

Achilles Prideaux placed both hands on the curve of his walking stick, which from past experience I knew to contain a hidden blade at the tip for protection, and held it in front of him, positioning it between us. "Because, Mademoiselle Beckingham, I wish to assist you in your search."

Even with all of the unexpected events that had transpired in my life in the weeks preceding this moment—the explosion, Ruby Stratton's murder, moving in with the Beckinghams, being attacked by Everilda—I still found myself shocked by Monsieur Prideaux's words. He had told me earlier that he would not help me in my search and I had believed him wholly.

"Why have you changed your mind?" I asked, the words coming out in a sigh.

He smiled at me, his thin mustache stretching wide across his face. "Because I spoke hastily before. The truth is, I am always available to help a friend."

I ran my hands down my olive-green tea dress, smoothing out the imaginary wrinkles before looking up at him. He really was a handsome man. His tan skin and slicked back hair complimented his looks nicely, if only he'd shave that horrid mustache.

I stepped towards him, hand extended, and he stepped forward to meet me, our hands clasping and shaking once.

Just then, Mr. Jacobsen reappeared in the doorway and his eyes widened at the sight of Monsieur Prideaux. "Miss Rose?" he asked warily, checking to be sure I was all right.

"The house is lovely," I said, releasing Monsieur Prideaux's hand. "I would be happy to call it home."

Mr. Jacobsen's nervousness dissipated at once as he clapped his hands in delight. "That is wonderful. And I'm sorry," he said, turning towards Achilles. "We haven't been introduced yet."

"This is Monsieur Achilles Prideaux," I said, placing a hand on Achilles shoulder and looking up at him. I met Monsieur Prideaux's gaze with a wink and the overwhelming feeling that my adventures in London were only just beginning. "He's a dear friend."

Continue following the mysterious adventures of Rose Beckingham in "A Cunning Death."

EXCERPT

FROM "A CUNNING DEATH: A ROSE BECKINGHAM MURDER
MYSTERY, BOOK 3."

First, I heard nothing. Then, slowly, a tinny ringing grew louder and louder until my entire body vibrated with it. I blinked against the gray haze in front of me, wondering whether I was somehow underwater. My chest felt impossibly heavy and it took several strong gasps before I could swallow any air. Each breath was acrid and ashy, burning my esophagus and scorching my lungs. I leaned forward, trying to get away from the fumes, and my face hit something solid. I reached for it and felt the hot leather upholstery of the front seat of the car.

Suddenly, everything came back to me all at once. The Beckinghams sharing the front seat with their driver, while Rose and I claimed the back. We were in Simla. At least, we had been...

Had I fallen asleep? That must have been it. I'd fallen asleep on the drive and was having a nightmare. I blinked hard in an attempt to wake myself up, but it didn't work. The smoke made my eyes water and I could feel tears streaming down my dusty cheeks.

"Rose?" I called, sliding my hand across the seat in search of my friend. "Mrs. Beckingham? Mr. Beckingham?"

I listened for their voices, but I couldn't hear anything aside from the sizzle of a nearby fire and the sound of someone coughing. Me. I was coughing.

"We will get you out, miss!"

There. Someone could hear me. I looked towards the direction of the voice and saw daylight streaming through what must have been the car window. Smoke and dust didn't allow me to see very far, but I could see human shapes moving around the vehicle.

Again, a flash of memory. A man moving through the crowd, arm pulled behind his head, a scowl on his face. The crowded streets near the market place pressed against our car, making it almost impossible to distinguish individual people from the mass, but this man had made himself obvious. He'd jumped around people, dodging arms and legs as he headed straight for us. I'd watched him with a curious eye, but didn't notice anything amiss until he swung his arm forward and released something.

With all the force of the initial blast, the horrifying truth came back to me.

Mrs. Beckingham gave a small yelp as the device landed inside the vehicle, Mr. Beckingham began to reach for it, Rose turned towards the commotion. My eyes, however, never left the man who had thrown the explosive. I watched as, content that his mission had been completed, he turned away from the car and disappeared back into the crowd. Then, darkness.

"Rose?" I shouted again, louder this time. "Answer me, Rose."

The car door opened, and a sticky breeze rolled through the opening, dispersing some of the smoke. It was as though someone had pulled back a curtain. I could see the seat in front of me, gouged and dripping with something sticky. I didn't linger on the sight, turning instead to where Rose had been sitting only a few minutes before. The seat was empty.

I could hear the sharp sounds of metal on metal coming from outside the car, and dusty silhouettes moved just outside the window. They were entreating me to calm down, to relax, to wait for help, but I leaned forward and swept my hand across the seat. I needed to find Rose.

Immediately, my hand landed in something warm and thick. I pulled back and held my hand up to the limited light coming through the door. Red dripped from my fingers, rolling down my wrist. I didn't need to think about what it was. I knew.

The contents of my stomach threatened to reappear, and I swallowed them down. I tried to take deep breaths, but the air was too thick. Everything felt wrong. The entire world had turned to chaos.

I looked back to where Rose should have been sitting, and for the first time, I saw something. A hand resting on the edge of the seat, as if Rose had simply slipped down to the floor between the front and back seats and was trying to pull herself back up.

I reached for her hand, wanting to help her, but in the brief second before our hands connected, I pulled back.

She wore a cheap metal ring with a fake jewel in the center. I'd bought it at a street market a few weeks before and had only recently given it to Rose. It was now the only thing that allowed me to identify the hand as hers, as it was no longer attached to her body. Where it should have connected to her arm, there was only mangled flesh and blood.

My mouth opened in a scream, but nothing came out. I

shouted for help, for Rose, for the hands of time to turn
back and undo the tragedy that had befallen my best friend,
but nothing happened. Then, I slipped into darkness.

My sheets and nightgown were soaked through with sweat. I
wiped my hand across my forehead and then placed it in my
lap, looking at the way my hand tapered down to my wrist.
At the way the delicate bones ran from my wrist up to my
elbow and to my shoulder. I'd never thought to be grateful
for the everyday mechanics of my body, but in that moment,
I was so relieved to find my hand firmly attached to the rest
of me.

I'd had to wash my sheets too many times to count since
moving into my new London home. Something about living
alone had brought the nightmares of the Simla explosion
back to the forefront of my mind. They were more vivid,
more enduring. On the ship from Bombay to London and at
Ashton House, I'd been able to rouse myself from the
dreams, but now I had to live the entire experience over
again before my subconscious mind would release me. I
woke several times a week in a pool of my own sweat, heart
pounding in my ears, eyes wide and searching for a glimpse
of the man who had ended the lives of the people I'd called
family for the better part of ten years.

I kicked my blankets down to the end of the bed and
swung my feet over the side. If the last few nights were to be
any judge, sleep would be elusive now that I'd woken up. I
tried to step carefully across the wooden floor. Aseem slept
in the servant's quarters, which were located just below my
bedroom, and my sleeplessness had begun to worry him.

It felt strange to be worried about by a twelve-year-old,

but I'd known since the moment I'd seen him aboard the *RMS Star of India* that he was wise beyond his years. And most importantly, Aseem was loyal. He made an incredibly useful errand boy and he asked few questions, which, in my opinion, was one of his best qualities. Still, if he heard me walking around in the middle of the night, he would mention it over breakfast and insist I take an afternoon nap.

I tip-toed to the curtains and pulled them back, letting in the moonlight. I'd assumed it was still the middle of the night, so I was surprised to see the beginnings of color leaching over the horizon. The sun would rise within the next hour, meaning I'd slept longer than I had all week.

I loved the view from my bedroom window, and found myself standing there, enjoying it frequently. Never in my life would I have thought I'd have my own house, especially not one so nice. But ever since I'd shed my old identity and stepped into the life of my dearly departed friend Rose Beckingham, doors I'd never even known existed were opening to me. With her inheritance, even though I had to collect it in monthly installments, I had a level of independence I'd never dreamed of. And more than that, I had the means to finally solve the mystery that had been plaguing me since I first left New York as a child: what had happened to my missing brother?

Something on the street below my window caught my attention, and I squinted down into the early morning darkness. A figure, a man in a long coat and a hat, lurked beneath a streetlight, standing just at the edge of the circle of light so his face was hidden in shadow. His shoulders were squared with my window, and based on the angle of his neck, I could tell he was looking up at me.

Startled, I stepped away from the window and back into the privacy of my room. I squeezed my eyes closed. Perhaps

I was still dreaming. I shook my head and then resumed my position at the window. I glanced down hesitantly, and the man was still there. My pulse quickened.

Before I could do anything other than stare down at him in confusion and growing fear, he bowed slightly at the hips, tipped his hat at me, and walked away down the sidewalk. I watched him disappear when he turned at the end of the block.

As soon as he was gone, the terror that had gripped me at the sight of him began to fade, replaced with a flurry of questions. Who was the man? What did he want? What would he have done had I not chosen that moment to go to my window?

A chill ran through me. I didn't know the man's true intentions, but I knew enough to feel threatened. He had tipped his hat to me before leaving. He wanted me to know that he knew I'd seen him, and he wanted me to realize that he didn't care.

I pulled the curtains closed and moved to sit on the edge of my bed. Even if I'd still been tired, it would have been impossible for me to fall asleep. Between the nightmares and the mysterious man, my brain was operating at full speed. I just didn't want to move downstairs and begin the day so early because it would force the rest of the house to wake up, as well. Though I told Aseem and George, my driver, I was more than capable of doing things on my own, they each woke up as soon as I did, which meant we'd all been getting a rather early start since moving into the new house.

I sat on the edge of my bed long enough that I had almost convinced myself the man at my window had been a continuation of my nightmare. I'd been in the flux space between dreaming and waking, and the man had been nothing more than a figment.

When I finally went down for breakfast, however, and Aseem handed me an unmarked box that had been left on the sidewalk outside, I knew the man had been all too real.

"You didn't see who left it?" I asked, taking the box from his hands and setting it on the dining room table.

Aseem shook his head, his dark brown eyes wide and honest. "No, Miss Rose. I went outside this morning and it was sitting in the middle of the sidewalk."

I studied the box without touching it. Though I had seen Aseem carry it in rather roughly, part of me still felt as though it would explode at the slightest touch. Though, perhaps that had more to do with what had transpired in India than any real cause for concern.

"Were you expecting something?" he asked.

"No, I wasn't, but thank you for bring this to me." I nodded my head and Aseem, astute for his young age, took that as his cue to leave. He carefully pulled the dining room doors closed behind him, leaving me alone with the box.

I studied the package for a few more seconds. It appeared to be innocuous. Medium-sized, roughly the size of a dinner plate, and wrapped in plain brown paper, it could have come from anywhere and been meant for anyone. Yet, somehow, I knew it was intended for me. The man standing outside my window had meant for me to see him lurking there. He meant for me to find this package. Despite an overwhelming urge to throw the box into the fire and go about my day as though the entire incident had never happened, I knew I wouldn't be able to rest until I knew what secrets the box contained. So, steeling myself, I moved forward, slipping my finger beneath the careful wrapping, and tore it open.

Sitting in the perfect center of the box was a chess piece. A pawn, to be exact. I had never been any good at chess and I'd played very infrequently, but still I recognized the piece. Beneath the pawn was a thick card folded in half. Without touching the pawn, I grabbed the card and slipped it from the bottom of the box. Unfolding it, I began to read.

Miss Dennet,

I hope you will not mind my use of your previous name. I do not fancy pretenses, and calling you Rose Beckingham would be a pretense of the falsest kind. As my greeting has no doubt made you aware, I am familiar with your story. Your investigation into the recent murder of Frederick Grossmith brought you to my attention. I was impressed with your handling of the case and sought to understand why an heiress would busy herself with the death of a man of no importance. The answer to that question lead me to the truth that you are not an heiress, but a pretender.

If you find yourself frightened at my knowing your secret, I urge you to be calm. I do not intend to share my knowledge with anyone. In fact, I wish to share some knowledge with you. If you are able to earn it.

In my research into you and your purpose here in London, I learned of your search for your long-lost brother, Jimmy. I hold a key piece of the puzzle that could lead you to Jimmy. The piece is yours should you choose to put your detective skills to work and solve a crime for me.

A person will be murdered this weekend in Somerset. If you can apprehend the killer after the crime has been committed, the information I have will be yours.

I eagerly await your decision.

"And you did not see the person's face?" Achilles Prideaux asked, pouring me a cup of tea.

I shook my head. "No, I only saw a shadowy figure and then I awoke to the mysterious package."

"And there was nothing distinctive about the package?"

I thought back on it, trying to recall any other details, but there was nothing. "Nothing aside from ordinary wrapping paper. It was not even addressed."

"How do you know it was meant for you, then?" Achilles asked.

"Because of the letter inside." I did not tell Monsieur Prideaux that the letter was addressed to my true identity, Nellie Dennet, and not to Rose Beckingham, but that hardly mattered. In either case, I was the intended recipient.

Achilles sat down in the chair across from me and folded his hands on the table in front of him. "Tell me everything again."

I'd tried to keep the mysterious package to myself, not wanting to worry anyone in my household with its contents, but it had proven to be impossible. Whoever had sent it knew my true identity, and they forewarned me of a murder. Wasn't it my duty, then, to report it? I wanted to take the matter to the police, but I could not do that without showing them the letter. And I could not show anyone the letter without revealing my secret and announcing to the world that I was not Rose Beckingham. So, I'd gone to Achilles Prideaux. Although he was a detective, he was a private detective, which meant I was not required to show or tell him anything I did not wish to. This fact had been proven when Achilles agreed to help me search for my brother,

Jimmy, despite the fact I had withheld from him that Jimmy was my brother. As far as Monsieur Prideaux knew, I had hired him to track down an old friend who had disappeared.

So, I'd left home just after breakfast and arrived at Achilles' house less than ten minutes later. I'd had no idea at the time I purchased my house how convenient it would be to live so close to a detective.

I repeated the story. I walked Monsieur Prideaux through waking from my nightmare, the shadowy figure below my window, the package Aseem found, and the letter and pawn inside. I left out all incriminating details that pointed to my true identity, and I had intentionally left the box and its contents at home, lest their examination by the detective reveal more of my own secrets than I wished him to guess.

When I finished, he leaned back in his chair and stared at the ceiling for so long I wondered whether he'd forgotten I was sitting across from him. I could tell Achilles was tired. He had just returned from a quick trip related to his detective work. His already tan skin looked to be a richer brown after days spent in the sun. He certainly stood out amongst the pale color palette of London. Light-skinned people, gray skies, pale stones. Though, Achilles didn't need any help standing out. His thin mustache gave him an air of mystery and the cane he carried, which I knew to hide a thin blade in the bottom, was an eye-catcher. He really was a handsome man. Except for that mustache. I would have shaved the mustache myself if I thought I could have done it before he'd realize.

"Well," I finally said, interrupting his thoughts. "What do you think I should do about the murder the sender mentioned?"

His mouth twisted to the side, the mustache twisting with it. "Nothing," he said firmly.

"Nothing?" I asked. "We have been warned about a possible murder and you want to do nothing about it?"

He shook his head. "I want *you* to do nothing about it. I want to investigate the sender of this message and see what information can be found."

"We have no clues with which to begin a search," I said. "We have no reason to believe any information can be found. Am I really supposed to sit by while an innocent person is murdered?"

"First, I have ways of finding things out," Achilles said, winking at me. "It is my job to solve the impossible. Second, we do not know the intended victim is innocent. You make too many assumptions, Mademoiselle, and I worry they will put you in danger."

"My life is not the one that was threatened," I reminded him. I did not like feeling as though I needed protecting. I'd found my way out of more than my fair share of life or death scrapes. Though, now that I was thinking about it, Achilles had helped me escape the first scrape and my cousin Edward had helped me escape the second. I shook my head, pushing the thought aside so I could focus on the matter at hand.

"This message could be a prank. If it is, there is no need to worry yourself about it or alarm the public. If it is not a prank, however," Achilles said, holding one finger in the air, "Then the person who sent you the package is obviously a criminal or has criminal ties. I know of no other way in which someone can be aware of an impending murder. In which case, accepting the challenge will only put you in danger."

"So, whether the person is a criminal or not, you do not want me to involve myself?" I asked for clarification.

"It is dangerous, Rose. I know you have had brushes with danger and murderers in the past and come away unharmed, but at some point, your luck will run out. And I, for one, do not wish to see any harm befall you."

I took a sip of my tea and returned the cup to the saucer. "Are you saying you are fond of me, Monsieur Prideaux?" I asked, raising an eyebrow and looking up at him.

Achilles looked suddenly nervous. He fidgeted in his seat, shifting from side to side, and then ran a finger along the length of his mustache. "It is my job to solve crimes. Should you die, I would no doubt be called upon to find your killer, and I have enough work to keep me busy as it is."

I grabbed my cream sweater from the back of the chair and slipped it on over my mauve buttoned blouse. "If I do find myself murdered, I'll do my best to schedule it for when your calendar isn't so full," I teased.

Achilles stood up and walked me towards his front door. "I certainly appreciate that, Mademoiselle Rose. Though, you should know that finding your murderer would be my top priority regardless of my schedule."

I was already on the steps, but I turned back to see him smiling at me. I wondered for the briefest of seconds whether this hadn't been the detective's attempt at flirting, but then he quickly warned me not to do anything with the information in the letter and slammed the door, killing the thought.

END OF EXCERPT

ABOUT THE AUTHOR

Blythe Baker is a thirty-something bottle redhead from the South Central part of the country. When she's not slinging words and creating new worlds and characters, she's acting as chauffeur to her children and head groomer to her household of beloved pets.

Blythe enjoys long walks with her dog on sweaty days, grubbing in her flower garden, cooking, and ruthlessly de-cluttering her overcrowded home. She also likes binge-watching mystery shows on TV and burying herself in books about murder.

To learn more about Blythe, visit her website and sign up for her newsletter at www.blythebaker.com